THE JOURNEY

CLARENCE M. DUNAWAY

The Journey
Copyright © 2023 by Clarence M. Dunaway

ISBN: 978-1639458127 (hc)
ISBN: 978-1639458080 (sc)
ISBN: 978-1639457366 (e)

All rights reserved. No part of this publication may be reproduced, distributed, or transmitted in any form or by any means, including photocopying, recording, or other electronic or mechanical methods, without the prior written permission of the publisher, except in the case brief quotations embodied in critical reviews and other noncommercial uses permitted by copyright law.

The views expressed in this book are solely those of the author and do not necessarily reflect the views of the publisher, and the publisher hereby disclaims any responsibility for them.

Writers' Branding
(877) 608-6550
www.writersbranding.com
media@writersbranding.com

CONTENTS

Chapter 1. Meet the Fletchers 5
Chapter 2. Fun in The Sun 22
Chapter 3. A little vacation 31
Chapter 4. Hi Ho Silver 45
Chapter 5. A miracle for Marla 58
Chapter 6. Marla Moves In 71
Chapter 7. A Possible Boyfriend 84
Chapter 8. Moving FORWARD 98
Chapter 9. A Hunting We Will Go 112
Chapter 10. No Surprises Here 126
Chapter 11. A little hair off the Dog 141
Chapter 12. To Catch A thief 155
Chapter 13. Man, On the Run 169
Chapter 14. The Capture 180

CHAPTER 1

MEET THE FLETCHERS

The Fletcher's lived in a gated community at the north side of Pleasantville, a relatively average size town located in the mountains north of Sacramento California. Ted and Martha Fletcher often dated in high school. Six months after graduation they got married. They settled down and raised two children. A son born in 1960, named Tom. It's unknown why they didn't name him Ted Junior, but Tom was a well-known name and they were satisfied with it. They could have called him Bubba, but Tom was less embarrassing. Three years later a girl was born they named her Marla.

Tom, like his father, married his high school sweetheart and moved from Pleasantville to Elko Nevada. He went to work for the Western Pacific Railroad as a fireman on a diesel electric, pretty easy job actually, and the benefits were great especially after retirement. Tom and Charlotte, Tom's wife had two children and just like Tom's parents they had a boy and a girl.

Elko Nevada is a relatively small Western town, unfortunately it was a gambling town like most towns in Nevada and it came equipped with three casinos. Fortunately, the family was not prone to gambling. It's a strange thing but most people that actually live in Nevada don't gamble. I guess they are smarter than the tourists.

Meanwhile back in California Marla was in her senior year in high school. However, unlike her parents and her brother she had no immediate desire to get married, she wanted to go to college striving to be a nurse. She was very pretty, but also level headed and she enjoyed helping people and what a better way to accomplish her than nursing.

Mr. Fletcher owned a prominent real estate business, and fortunately could afford to help his daughter with her college tuition. However, she chose to live at home with Brenda, her best friend since the fifth grade. Brenda was somewhat less fortunate and had to work in order to support herself. So, consequently she lived with her parents as well only her choice was out of necessity.

Brenda worked at Frank's bar and grill from 5PM to 11PM and being 18, she was too young to serve alcohol and waiting tables wasn't something Brenda wanted to waste the rest of her life doing. Nursing was also her thing. She was anxious to get started, but it seems the more she wanted to rush into her occupation the slower time went. (Hang in there Brenda your time will come faster than you think) she, too, was a beautiful dark-haired blue-eyed girl and to reach her life goal as with Marla, they both had to be patient and fend off the males as much as possible. If either were to fall in love in all likelihood their dreams would shatter. It happens all too often where young people spend two or even four years of their lives in college only to get married and throw away their dreams and never reach their goals. It was going to be difficult for the two, but somehow things seemed to work out in the end.

The college was only about 2 miles from where Brenda lived, 3 miles perhaps from where Marla's parents lived. However, Marla could have lived in the dorm her parents could afford, but she wanted to continue to live with her parents and save them money, even if they didn't need it.

Thanksgiving, 1984, only a year after, Tom and his family moved to Elko Nevada. Of course, Marla was there but without her friend Brenda, she too had a family and was expected to be with them on the holidays. It was only a short time later that Tom and his family showed up, so now it was party time. The Fletcher family all gathered around the table and held hands while Mrs. Fletcher said grace. At the conclusion of the prayer she said, "Okay Ted pour the wine while I get the bread from the oven."

After passing different dishes around the table each takes a portion on their plates.

Tom began telling a story about when he first moved to Elko he was hired on the Western Pacific Railroad as a fireman. "However, before I could work on my first trip, we had to make what they called a round robin. I just rode along and watched what the firemen were doing, after all this was a learning experience. Nick, a friend of mine that I met in Elko he, too, was hired on as a fireman. We boarded the train early one morning in Elko and headed out on our journey to complete our training. Our first stop was Winnemucca but only temporarily, and then on to Porterville which was the end of the trip. It Just so happened that Nick's father lived in Porterville and was also an engineer on the WP. Since we didn't have to be back to Elko at any particular time, Nick's father asked us to stay over so that he would take us to Reno for dinner and a show. We agreed, "we might as well have a little fun on this cruise" said Nick, so stay over we did.

Nick's father drove us to Reno, and we went to a large hotel set just above the feather River that flows through the town. Up on the top floor we had dinner and were entertained by some guy named Jeffries. I'd heard of him before, but this is the first I'd ever seen the good singer. We enjoyed his music. The dinner was also great. After dinner and the show, we headed back to Portola and into bed because Nick and I had to get up early in the morning to catch the WP back to Elko.

Funny part about this orientation and learning process was the book of rules. It seemed sort of ridiculous. We had to read this book of rules which is a small book with a lot of pages. The ridiculous part about it was you really didn't have to read the book at all. It was just a legality because anytime we wanted to quit reading, we could stop just sign the back page, and turn it in and we were in like Flynn. This protected the railroad from a lawsuit because we signed as though we had read the book rules and knew all about what we were doing. So, if we caused an accident or injured ourselves or anybody else it wouldn't fall back on the railroad.

At 8:05 am the WP rolled into the Porterville station. We were sitting there on the bench waiting. We climbed aboard and were off like her turtles back to Elko and I mean a herd of turtles. A freight train pulling 86 cars doesn't exactly break many speed limits.

We made another quick stop in Winnemucca and then onwards towards Elko which put us in the middle of the round robin in the dead of night. Fortunately, I had a warm cozy bed waiting for me along with the lovely wife. Tom's wife, Charlotte, looks over and gives him a smile. I think she liked the compliment.

Two days passed and I went to the station at 8:30 AM to check the bulletin board to see if we were going to get a trip with me as a fireman, but of course that wasn't possible. We still had half the round robin to complete but I checked it anyhow.

Nick and I boarded the train in Elko at 8:00 AM sharp the next morning on our last round of the trip and the completion of our training.

We were on our way to Wendover stopping in a little town called Wells about halfway there and then onwards to Wendover.

Since we had no rules at this time, we were allowed to do anything we wanted to, so Nick said, 'Let's continue on to Salt Lake City,' since neither of us had ever been there. After spending the night in a motel and circumventing the city like the tourists we were. We grabbed an early morning run back towards Elko."

Ted, Tom's father, interrupted, "is there an end to this oratory, the food's getting cold."

Tom returned with, "You don't have to stop eating, you're not eating with your ears besides," I'm just about to reach the climax of my story.

Nick and I hung around Elko for a couple of days checking the board everyday just in case one of our names were on it. It so happened my name popped up on the board. It seems I would be taking over the 4:05 PM train and relieving the firemen, this time it was for real. I will be on my own and responsible for anything it might take place in the process.

I did my job, at least I thought I did. I checked the oil, water gauge and fuses that had to be done before the firemen on deck could be released from his duties. He followed me through every test until he was satisfied that everything checked out. He slapped me gently on the shoulder and said, 'good luck,' and he disembarked from the train. Needless to say, I was a little shaky being the first trip I was going to try very hard not to make any mistakes I mean, I didn't want to get fired on the first trip, actually my first day of work as a fireman.

My run as they call it from Elko to Wendover where I would spend the night paid for by the WP. Well I gotta say it wasn't much of a night's sleep for one thing the motel was almost on the railroad tracks every time a train would come through it would rattle your cage.

We had only been in bed for about three hours. It was 1:30 AM when they woke us up and told us we were taking the next train back to Elko. For one reason or another and I don't know what it was, but we had to relieve the crew and take over their shift back to Elko.

Wendover was situated very close to the Utah border, in fact it was the last town in Nevada before you got into Utah.

We had 87 freight cars with four engines to pull them and two more behind caboose to help us over the hump. There's a small stop 16 miles from Wendover called Shatner that had water tanks to fill the engines when they got to that point. There were 8 miles of 6° grade on the way up the hill to Shafter and that was the reason for the extra two engines.

I went through the routine with the firemen checking the water gauge and the fireman was right there looking over my shoulder. The tanks seemed to be full, so I checked the oil. It too was ok, plenty of oil there, no foreseeable problems except I was sleepy. I climbed up in the cab besides the hog head, (engineer) and we were off like a herd of turtles, believe me. We were 2 miles out of Wendover and one of the lights came on overhead above my seat indicating we were low on water. It seemed to blow the roof off the cab because water and steam was shooting up in the air everywhere, mostly steam. Obviously when I checked the gauge there was pressure holding water up in the gauge so I couldn't tell, it looked to me like it was full.

I shut the engine down and went back to the cab, got my ass chewed by the engineer. I apologized saying, "I checked it, boss it showed that we had plenty of water as confirmed by the firemen" I was relieved. Well, if that wasn't bad enough two miles further another engine shut down for the same reason, what's the odds?

Needless to say, I was the most unpopular fireman on the railroad. It took us almost 16 hours to get to wells, and 16 hours is the maximum amount of time you're allowed to work according to railroad rules.

When we pulled into the station at Wells Nevada there was a station wagon waiting there for us, it looked like we got to ride in luxury for the next 50 miles. We even got double pay, however that didn't make the crew happy enough because no one said a word to me the whole trip. I guess they were a little pissed at me and I couldn't understand why after all I got them double time, what else did they want?

It was quiet around the railroad station in Elko for a few days. My only friend was Nick and he was out on a run. I only hope he did better than I did. So that's what happened. I thought perhaps you'd be interested in my little miserable tale of woe." Tom finally concluded his story. Just as a joke everyone at the table applauded, I don't think it was the interest in the story it was more the fact that he'd finished it, now they could move on with what they were there for, a fabulous turkey dinner.

Thanksgiving finally came to an end and Tommy's family headed back to Elko; Marla returned to college.

Five years past, the girls finish college and one year of nursing. Both were fortunate to get jobs at the local hospital. The training was a great experience and they learned well. It wasn't long before they both became popular with the hospital staff and all the nurses. Marla and Brenda were now beginning to enjoy the surroundings.

Brenda was still working at Frank's bar and grill only now she tended bar no more waiting tables. She found herself in a position where she could socialize more. When a young man sat down at the bar Brenda would converse with the customers and things became interesting. She was too busy before while waiting tables to stop and grab.

Customers had different stories to tell, or perhaps more of a come on than anything else, but it worked. In the late hours after the diner closed and the customers dwindled down to a precious few, Brenda would have a drink with male customers as well as her female friends, they would talk for hours. She soon found herself being drawn into the very situations she had been fighting off for the past three years. She had dated before, but she was very cautious not to get too close she wasn't ready for love, but it would invariably happen in spite of her resistance Brenda had a cousin that lived in Dallas Texas and worked as a nurse at the health Presbyterian Hospital Dallas. Kathy, Brenda's cousin would write to her at least once a week, they were very close.

Brenda's cousin, in one of her letters mentioned that there would be an opening at the hospital where she worked, and she was positive that she could get the job for her. She even alluded to the amount of pay Brenda would get and it was much more than she was getting now working two jobs. However, she might have to obtain a Texas license.

Brenda gave the offer a great deal of consideration although she loved her position and didn't want to leave Marla behind, they were such good friends. Brenda while working with Marla asked her to come to the bar with her after work so that she had something she wanted to discuss with her and perhaps have a drink or two?

After her shift at the hospital, Brenda drove her car with Marla close behind in her own car. Brenda parked her car behind the bar and grill, got out of the car and waited for Marla who pulled in and parked alongside. They walked together into the bar through the rear door surprising Frank who was behind the bar.

Frank greeted the two young ladies well, motioning them to the bar and having a seat. "What can I get you ladies, I know what you drink Brenda, but I don't remember seeing your friend Marla here more than half a dozen times, she's never had more than one drink and that was usually ginger ale?"

"Well," Marla said, "just what would you recommend for an occasional drinker?"

"Oh, let me see," Frank said, scratching his forehead, "do you like orange juice?" Thinking perhaps a screwdriver.

"Not sure," she responded, "too much acid."

Frank mixed Brenda's drink while attempting to conjure up something Marla might enjoy. He walked to the back of the bar nodding his head up and down as though he had reached a conclusion. Frank reached up and grabbed the tallest bottle from the top shelf and poured it into what appeared to be a pregnant thimble, "try this and tell me what you think?" Frank challenged.

Marla looked at the little glass saying, "if I like it would it come in a bigger glass?"

"Well, just try the one in front of you and I'll explain it to you." He challenged again.

"Wow," Marla said after a small sip from the tiny glass, "this is really good, but what do you call it, a teaser?" She snickered.

Brenda said, "it's liqueur and the reason for the little glass for one, it is a famous and delightful French drink, and if you think that's a small glass try an angel kiss it is really small." What your sampling is normal after drinking, not always.

"Well, thank you Frank but I bet you don't sell much of it do you?"

"No, not really it's for people that don't drink much or can't handle the strong power of alcohol. And most people use it as an after dinner drink!"

Frank walked away to wait on the customer at the far end of the bar.

Brenda pulled her stool closer to Marla's and said, "well here it goes, I have a cousin, you heard me speak of her, she writes me a letter every week and although we were separated by several miles, we were still very close. Anyway, I got a letter from her a couple of days ago. She works at the Presbyterian Hospital in Dallas, Texas.

She guaranteed me a job with her, and the salary is much more than I make working two jobs here. I'll be able to share her house and pay half the rent, sounds too good to turn down."

Marla was silent, took another sip of her drink trying to absorb all that Brenda had to say. "Well, what do you want me to say? Are you wanting my blessings? I couldn't possibly ask you to turn your back from a position like that, although I love you like a sister, always have, but you need to follow your dreams. We will always remain friends, and who knows I might even fly to Dallas on my vacation and spend it with you girls in fact I can guarantee it."

Brenda said, "I expected a little more resistance, but I love you for respecting my decisions, wish you could come with me."

"I'm afraid that's not possible at this time. You know my mother's having a heart problem. I'd feel terrible if I left and anything happened to her, we'll see how things go. Do you have any idea when you might leave on your new journey?" Marla questioned.

"No," Brenda replied, "I still have to talk to my cousin to make sure of the date and when I can start work. I don't want to drive a thousand miles only to be idle for a week, or for a month I'm ready to work. I'll let you know as soon as I find out. Okay? And I have to check how long it will take me to get a Texas license."

"Well" Marla said, "give us enough time to throw you a go away party. I'm sure some of the nurses at the hospital want to be included in the festivities. You know you've made a lot of friends since you've been there, I'm sure they wouldn't want you to sneak out the back door never to know what happened."

Frank spoke up, "I'll tell you what, Thursdays are pretty slow around here. Maybe we can plan on having your party here, I'll post a sign a day in advance saying to our faithful friends that we're closing Thursday night only. Will reopen on Friday, an important nurses' ball and farewell party. What do you think about that?"

"That would be perfect, Frank!" Brenda said, "but are you sure you wouldn't lose some customers? I mean although Thursday nights are slow you still have regulars you wouldn't want you to lose any of them because of me. Let's wait until I get an affirmation from my cousin then we can decide, okay?" Brenda concludes with a question.

They all agreed to wait for confirmation, then they said good night Frank.

Brenda and Marla left the bar through the rear door into the parking lot.

Marla said, "I'll see you at work in the morning," as she pulled out of the lot and slowly drove away.

Almost 7:30 AM a teenager crossing the street at the crosswalk was suddenly struck down by a fast-moving car that ignored the red light, never even slowed down. A witness took down a partial license number but could only get a portion GC and possibly the number six. It's too bad the car was moving so set fast she might've got the entire license plate number that would make it much easier to track down. Unfortunately, cell phones were not yet available however, another car driving along the same route seeing what happened stopped at the nearest phone booth and called 911. Soon there were sirens and flashing lights screaming down the road towards the accident.

The ambulance pulled up to where the young boy lay on the street. Two attendants jumped out the rear door of the ambulance and pulled the gurney out the strap the lad the gurney and sped away to the hospital sirens screaming.

The police pushed the onlookers aside and began asking questions looking for the person that saw the car hit the boy and sped away. She told the officer what she witnessed but it was of little help. The police officer asked her what make the car was. She responded with, "all I know it was a light-colored car, a sedan I think, but I can't tell you the make, I am afraid I'm not very good at identifying make models of vehicles." "Well" said Sgt. Ed Baker, the lead detective, "thank you ma'am for the information." Shortly after he dismissed the lady, Sgt. got a call from Lieut. Kelly at the police headquarters. He told Sgt. Baker that an all-night drugstore had been robbed just two blocks away and only a few minutes earlier. The Sgt. turned to the officer standing next to him, telling him what had transpired just minutes ago as per Detective Kelly.

"I guess it's pretty obvious what happened, it appears to me that the robber was in a hurry to get away and nothing was going to stand in his way, not even a pedestrian."

"I think you're right Charlie, call the Station and have them contact the radio and television stations around the city and ask them to put the word out asking for citizens that may have any knowledge of the accident to please contact the police department. Tell them, especially around the neighborhood, to be on the lookout for a light-colored sedan either light gray or silver color, with possible blood on the front fender of the car or perhaps even the bumper."

"Okay, Ed. I'm on it." returned the officer, "this was going to be somewhat difficult giving the miniscule amount of description I only wish she could've got more of the license plate number we might have had a heck of a lot better chance of identifying the car."

Marla and Brenda pulled into the hospital parking lot simultaneously almost as if they planned it. They greeted each other with a hello and a hug. The two girls walked towards the entrance to the hospital. When they approached the main floor, they noticed lots of activity in front of room 306. The two stood there looking through the window into the room where doctors and nurses were scrambling all over the place.

The attending physician looked towards the glass window from inside the room and noticed Marla. He immediately motioned for her to enter the room. He appeared to be very anxious that she had yet to get into her uniform, But I guess the patient was more important than the uniform.

Dr. Malloy worked with Marla on many cases that's why he selected her to assist him, he then dismissed a couple of the other nurses. The doctor began to explain what happened, "this young lad had just arrived here and was in a terrible condition. He's a victim of a hit-and-run, and they really did a number on him."

She asked, "what would you want me to do?"

"Well, start by cleaning him up then start a regiment of blood AB negative and also saline. If we're out of AB negative you know that type O works, so get started. The doctor ordered, "I'm afraid the youngster doesn't stand a very good chance of survival, but we have to do our best to try and get him stabilized."

Marla had worked on many organ transplants with Dr. Malloy that's why he had so much confidence in her.

After Marla finished her job getting the patient clean and added all the survival attachments, she stood looking down on the young man remembering her brother when he was that age. She began to tear up and that is something the nurse is not supposed to do and that's a get too close to the patient. You can't afford to make it personal or you will never become a good nurse. In spite of all the efforts from the doctors and nurses the young lad died.

Marla went to the lounge, and Dr. Malloy reminded her of the rules about making patient's personal.

She met Brenda in the hall, she too tried to console and comfort Marla and also said, "remember you can't make a patient your personal assignment. You have enough problems without taking on everyone else's." They turned and walked away in different directions.

Life went on, Brenda still worked at Frank's bar and grill.

While at the police station a tip came in on the wanted vehicle involved in the accident. However, what was then a felony, is now a homicide.

The Tip that came into the Police Department was information where the car was located, the officer at the station passed the information on to Sgt. Baker.

Ed Baker said, "Okay Roy, let's go see if this is the right vehicle."

The two climbed into a squad car and drove together to the address where the car was parked along the curb.

Roy called the license number into the office, and said, "See if we can find the owner's name." The information came back in about 10 minutes. The car belonged to Charles T. Beckford.

Sgt. Baker said, "Let's go knock on the door and see if we can find out any more information and if the occupant owns the vehicle."

The two officers approached the front door. Couple of quick knocks on the door and they backed away and waited for an answer. Within a matter of seconds, a young lady opened the door and questioned what the two men wanted.

Sgt. Baker identified them as police officers showing a badge and asked if she was the owner of the vehicle parked in front of her house.

She said she had no knowledge of who it belonged to and that it had been there for a few days. She said, "I was about to call the police if it wasn't gone by this evening." The officers thanked her for her time and assistance then returned to their vehicle.

"Well Ed, I guess we're going to have to dig deeper to see if we can find this Beckford person. I have a feeling it's a stolen car."

"Yeah, you're probably right. There's nothing like making the situation more difficult. Call the station and have the car picked up, will have the lab check it out for fingerprints and perhaps the blood on the left front fender. I'm not sure how they can match it. All we can do is try."

Back in the 80s there was no way of checking blood samples for DNA, just the blood type making it difficult to match the victim's blood with the assailants.

The day finally came to an end for Brenda, the letter she's been waiting for, that is if she truly plans to move to Texas, it's now or never. According to her cousin, she would start on 22nd of May, which was just two weeks away. "I'd better call Marla and let her know" she thought silently to herself. She decided to drive to the Fletcher's home and tell them the information with the family while all together.

Brenda arrived at Marla's at 7:30 PM. It was Saturday so everyone should be home.

Marla had just pulled into the driveway and when Brenda pulled up behind her, set the parking brake and exited her vehicle.

Marla turned to face her with a question, "to what do I owe this privilege?"

"Oh, I don't know, I just thought I'd give you a break."

They laughed, Brenda reached out and took Marla by the hand, "how was your day I see you're still in scrubs, don't tell me you drew a Saturday shift?"

"Okay."

"What do you mean okay?"

"You asked me not to tell you, besides it should be obvious I don't usually go shopping in my uniform."

"Okay, if we're going to play games, are you going to invite me in, or should I just climb back in my car and go home?"

"Since when do you need an invitation?" Marla said laughing.

When they entered the house Marla's mother was in the kitchen preparing dinner, her father was in the den sitting in his favorite chair. When he saw Brenda, he said "well for evermore to what do we owe this pleasant surprise?"

"Is everyone in your family the same?"

"I'm going into the kitchen to see how Brenda is received by mom."

She walks into the kitchen where Mom stood next to the sink peeling potatoes. She looked up at Brenda and said, "well for heaven's sake, come here and give me a hug."

"At least this was a different greeting that I got from the other two." Brenda laughed well, squeezing Mrs. Fletcher around the waist.

"What in the world are you up to?" Mrs. Fletcher queried.

"About 5'8." Brenda returned.

They both begin to laugh, "you're sure in a silly mood." said Mrs. Fletcher.

"Yeah well, I'm a little crazy anyhow you know."

"Are you joining us for dinner?" Mrs. Fletcher asked.

"Well now that you ask, how could I turn down such a great offer?" She returned.

"Dinner will be on the table in about 10 minutes, go visit with dad, he enjoys your company."

"Are you saying you don't enjoy my company?" Brenda asked jokingly.

Mrs. Fletcher's last words were, "oh, get out of here."

Brenda went into the living room, dropped down on the divan next to Marla. "I guess you will be having a guest for dinner, Marla."

"Really, just who might that be?" Marla asked, knowing well who she meant.

"How about your best friend, do I have to remind you who that is?"

"Marla laughed saying," no, I only have one friend and her name is Brenda she said squeezing Brenda's hand. "Like a little wine before dinner? "Sure, why not I can't dance."

"What the hell has dancing got to do with drinking wine, you drink a glass almost every night, but I've never seen you dance around the room?"

"You're not with me all the time, you know sometimes I do silly things when you're not around."

Dad spoke up, "is this the way you girls entertain yourself all the time or is it just for my pleasure? And by the way I've got a good suggestion for you."

"Oh, oh, here it comes, just what have you conjured up in that over worked brain of yours?" Marla's question was a little touch of laughter.

Brenda chimed in, "yeah pops what's on your mind and do you really think you have a cure for our silliness?"

"I'm not sure about that, but I know something you haven't done for a long time. It might help out the situation. You know I still have that old tent out in the garage that I bought when your mom and I used to go camping all the time. It is just big enough for two, so I was thinking you might want to take that tent with some of my fishing gear and go up to Crystal Springs for a few days. You know Memorial Day is just around the corner and that would be a great time to go. You have three days and I'll bet you can take an extra day off if you want. I am sure your boss won't mind, and it may be the last time you two will see each other for a while, so what do you say?"

"Oh, I don't know," Marla said, "we haven't been up in the mountains for a longtime."

"What do you think about my idea Brenda?" Marla's father asked.

"Sounds like a wiener to me." Brenda came back with another silly answer; it didn't go unnoticed.

"Well here we go again. I thought the fun games were over with, but I guess it will continue on as long as you're here." Said Marla.

"Well, in all seriousness it sounds like a pretty good idea to me what you think I'm game if you are, we haven't done anything together for a long time and I think it would be a great idea to get away from the hustle and bustle for a few days. We might even run into a couple of handsome fishermen and bring them home with us, wouldn't that be great?"

"Allow me to ponder the plan for a couple of days and we'll talk about it again, maybe next time we meet you can come to my house for dinner and we'll talk about it over dinner and a glass of wine, you know we serve wine to my house as well."

Dinner was over, Brenda asked Mrs. Fletcher if she could help her with the dishes.

"Oh, get out of here, you're a guest and guests don't do dishes, not in my house." Mrs. Fletcher said almost as if you were insulted.

"Okay mom, your wish is my command." Brenda returned. "What do you say we have one more glass of wine before I retreat and head back to my dungeon?"

"Of course, Brenda but are you sure you can handle it? I mean this will be three glasses and you have to drive, you wouldn't want a DUI, would you? I mean it would mess up our up-and-coming camping trip?" Marla said, reminding her of the trip they're about to take.

"Well it appears to me as though you've made up your mind about the trip for both of us, don't I get a say in the matter?" Brenda responded by raising one eyebrow.

"Of course, you do it was just a warning I wouldn't want to see you in jail. You know it would go on your record as a felony and how would that look at the hospital having a drunk nurse?"

"Now you're getting downright nasty calling me a drunk, so now let's get down to reality and have that other glass of wine, would your dad care to join us?"

"Well, I see no reason why not. After all I'm not driving anywhere so let's have it, pour the wine, we'll get drunk as a skunk."

"Now, dad is not really going to get drunk and if she doesn't pass my test before she leaves here, she will have to spend the night! And that's that."

They sipped one more glass of wine and cut up making jokes and acting silly for another hour until it was time for Brenda to leave for home.

"Okay, Marla, what is this test you are going to perform before I leave? Is it anything like the cops do when they stop you and make you walk the line in front of the car trying to hold your balance? That's hard to do when you're sober, much less drunk. Or perhaps take a blood test, you're not planning on taking a blood test, are you?" Brenda said acting silly. I've got a better plan. I'll call home and tell them I will I'm spending the night with you, and we can have another glass, how does that sound?" Brenda asked but she was serious.

As it turned out dad had another glass of wine as well. Brenda stayed the night with Marla. Now they can cut up all night which they haven't done for several months.

CHAPTER 2

FUN IN THE SUN

The girls decided to take Marla's father seriously and take that trip to Crystal Springs on the holiday weekend which was only about 10 days away.

Marla's father suggested that she take his car because he had a SUV and it had more room than hers.

He said, "you take the SUV and if I need a car, I'll use yours. I may have to run to the office, but I don't know for sure so just in case, just leave the keys."

"Okay, dad. That would be great and thank you for the car suggestion and I'll take care of your car." She said while giving her dad a big hug. The Fletcher family has a great relationship.

Marla met Brenda at the hospital, Brenda was there early. She was scrubbing down in preparation for surgery.

"Good morning Brenda, you have a surgery on the docket this morning?" "Yes, Dr. Malloy asked me to assist him with the kidney transplant. It's a young girl. She's been waiting three months for a donor."

"Well, good luck. I have to see what's in store for me this morning. Oh, and by the way, my dad donated his SUV so we have plenty of space to haul everything we need."

"That's terrific Marla, that's great, it's obvious you are the apple of his eye."

I'm sure your dad feels the same way about you. I think it's because we're the only girls in the family. Fathers are like that, always calling us their little girl. Do you suppose this will continue when we are in our 50s?"

"I think it's nice being someone's little girl." Brenda said. "I've got to go to Marla, maybe I'll see you at lunch time."

"You're not suggesting eating in the cafeteria, are you?" Marla asked with a sheepish grin, nobody likes to eat in the hospital cafeteria.

"See you later, duty calls." Brenda said as she turned and walked away into the room where the doctor was waiting.

When she entered the room, the doctor looked up and said, "it's about time. Let's get her down to the operating room."

The two girls met after work, Brenda asked Marla to go with her to the bar for a glass of wine so that they could talk about the trip. Brenda was anxious to make the trip; the two girls haven't gone anywhere together in a long time. Brenda pulled into the parking lot; Marla was close behind. They entered through the rear door and found that there was a new, different, bartender. They wondered where Frank was and why he was behind the bar.

He looked up in surprise to see the girls, he had never seen them enter from the rear door before. "Why are you two coming through the rear door, it's only for employees," he declared.

"Well where is Frank, I work for him. I must be relieved, what's your name and why didn't Frank tell me about having a new bartender?" Brenda asked with a puzzled look on her face.

Oh, he said, "you must be Brenda. I'm afraid you startled me coming through the rear door. I didn't know the rules. Although I was expecting someone to show up, and here you are."

"Yes," Brenda replied, "and what might your name be?"

"Well, he returned. "It might be Bubba, but it isn't, it's Gordon," He answered.

All three laughed, I'm 30 minutes early, so my friend Marla and I are going to sit at a table and have a drink. By the way, where is Frank? He is always here when I show up for work."

"He was feeling a little down the dumps, so he asked me to come by and tend bar until you get here, he didn't tell me you were such a pretty bartender"

"Marla, I guess you heard his name is Gordon, a relief bartender." She said in the form of a question.

"Yeah, I heard, hey Gordon," she said like it was an introduction.

"Let's take a seat, I'm ready for that drink." "Okay Marla, bar or booth?" Brenda asked.

"I think I would prefer to sit at the booth, there's more room and privacy." "Good, go grab a couple of seats and I'll bring the drinks. What are we having tonight, wine, or do you have something else in mind?" Brenda asked. "I don't know, what is it you drink most of the time?"

"I think I'll have a margarita without salt. Watch Gordon's face when I order, and by the way, I'm ordering for both of us, is that all right?"

"Sure, you're the bartender, I'll try anything you think I can handle," Marla replied.

Brenda went to the bar, slipped her hand down over the bar top and said, "Gordon, make me two topless Maggie's."

"Sure, coming right up, what the hell is a topless Maggie?"

Brenda laughed, "it's a Margarita without salt on the rim of the glass." "Where the hell did you come up a title like that, and how many bartenders you know that you have a clue what you're talking about?"

"Well, whereas it's true, not many have ever heard the term, they always get a kick out of it."

Gordon poured two margaritas and set them on the bar. Brenda picked up the two glasses and said thanks, oh, and put it on my tab. She walked away where Marla was waiting patiently, gazing out the window into the dusk of night.

Brenda soon showed up, cradling two martinis. She set one in front of Marla, then set the other down across the table from her and took a seat.

Marla took a sip of her drink, and then commented on how good it tasted, "this is the first time I've ever had one of these Brenda, good choice."

"Yeah, I thought you might enjoy it. It's also my favorite." She declared. "Some of the drinks I see customers drinking must be painful by the faces

They gulp down the liquid." Marla commented.

"I never thought of it being painful, but it does sort of make sense. If you want to see real pain. Try running your arm through a 1940s Maytag wringer, now that's pain." Brenda said with a smile.

"What the heck made you come up with something like a 100-year-old wringer? And how would you know you were not around in those days, where you?" Marla asked with laughter.

"Fortunately, you're right. It was my mother that told me it happened to a six-year-old kid. He and a young girl next door were playing like they were doing the laundry and when the boy picked up a sock and started putting it in the wringer, thinking it was going to wring the water from the sock like he'd seen his mother do so many times. Unfortunately, the young lad's fingers got caught in the wringer and started pulling his hand in, he was screaming so loud that the woman next door, the mother of the little girl came running over and without thinking, put it in reverse. It was already up above his elbow, but she put it in reverse and let it roll all the way out when all the while there was a release on top of the wheels. All she has to do is reach up on top and hit it with her hand and it would've opened the both rollers and saved the poor kid a lot of misery."

"Well Brenda, I think we should start thinking about the upcoming trip. You know, we have plenty of room in the car and I think instead of hauling a small grill to cook on, we might as well buy a heavy screen that we can lay across the fire over the stones you're going to use to build the fireplace."

"What do you mean I'm going to build? What are you going to be doing while I'm making a fire pit?" Brenda asked.

"I thought we could both gather the rocks and then while you're building a fire pit I can start putting up the tent."

"Yeah, I guess that's fair enough, then when we finished with that chore, we could both gather firewood.

"Sounds like a plan, I can hardly wait. It's been a long time since you and I have been alone together, and I guess I'm getting somewhat anxious.

"Well, I suppose I'd better relieve the bartender so he can do whatever he does when he's not working."

"Okay, as soon as I finish my drink I'm going to head out, if I hurry, I might make it home in time for dinner. When she got up just for laughs, she left the dollar tip before leaving the diner. I might make it home in time for dinner."

Marla pulled into her driveway, got out of the car and entered the house. When she opened the door, her mother was on her way into the kitchen. She walks over to her mother and gives her a hug," hi mom how are you doing?" She asked.

"I'm fine sweetheart, you're just in time for dinner. Come on in the kitchen, sit down, your father will be here in a moment."

"I hope you made enough to feed four, I'm hungry enough to eat a bear." Marla said jokingly.

The three gathered around the table, mom said grace after which came three voices saying, "amen." They begin to pass plates around the table, each one taking a helping hand and passing the plate onto the next person.

Mr. Fletcher asked Marla if she and Brenda had decided what they would take on the trip.

Marla said that they had a conversation about it at the grill just before she came home, "it seems everything is set to go."

Marla, got a call from the hospital asking her if she could come in and pull another shift, that two of the nurses called in sick and they were having a busy night."

"Well mom, I have to go back to the hospital, looks like I will be home in the early morning, by the way mom dinner was great."

"Oh, get out of here, it was not any better than it is any other night, I always cook the same as I have been all my life." Mom Fletcher said, knowing her daughter was pulling your leg.

When Marla reached the hospital. It looked like a war zone. People were running around like chickens with their heads cut off, nurses running back and forth across the hall to the surgical room and back to the conference room.

"What happened?" Marla asked.

"There was a small plane crash, two dead, three more badly injured and were short of staff, and it's raising havoc around here. Might as well get into your scrubs it looks like you're going to be here for a while, long while afraid." The nurses are running a marathon instead of a shift.

The injured were from middle-aged to youngsters. Some were just hanging on by a thread from broken bones to head trauma, Marla would do the best she could to save them all.

She put her uniform on, scrubbed her hands and went to work on a young lady, she appeared to be injured more than the others. She asked a male nurse to have the patients brought up from the emergency room up to the OR and assign nurses to each patient.

Most of the surgeries went well, all survived, however, for some would need many more follow ups and surgeries before they would be back to normal as one might hope.

Marla wanted to collaborate with Brenda to see how much longer she had to work thinking they could leave at the same time. However, Brenda was in the middle of an operation, it appeared there would be no time to converse. She found out that Brenda would be at least two hours, Marla gave up the idea of waiting around so she went to the locker room, showered and put on her street clothes.

Marla climbed behind the wheel of her car, backed out and headed for home and a well needed rest. For some reason she thought there was someone following her, she's had this feeling before just a few nights ago. However, she chalked it up to imagination. She drove around the parking lot making her way to the ground floor and out into the street. She pointed the car towards home She turned the car down Oak drive and proceeded towards home when she noticed there appeared to be following her. After turning the corner, the car behind her was moving at the same pace. She noticed the car turned as well. Marla was only a few blocks from her destination, she turned into her driveway and sat there watching the car following her as it proceeded down the street. The car turned into a driveway at the last house on the street, shut out the lights, climbed out of the car and entered the house. Marla felt like a fool, (Keep your eyes open Marla you look ravishing to any normal male.)

It was 4:30 in the morning when Marla climbed into her bed, exhausted from the double shift. I can only imagine how Brenda's going to feel, she pulled more than a double shift, nineteen hours in all.

Marla spent most of the day in bed, it would be time for dinner when she got up and hit the shower. She would have dinner with family before starting a night shift, 10 PM to 7:30 AM.

Marla met Brenda in the locker room where Marla was putting on her street clothes Brenda was dressing in her uniform.

They spoke briefly, discussing their up and coming trip. Brenda said, "Come by at Franks tonight, my shift will be complete at 8:00 PM, but I have to close Franks tonight, so I'll be up for a while."

"Okay," Marla agreed, "I have some shopping to do, then I'll go home for the rest of the day. I don't have to go to work until 8:00 in the morning." Her shopping trip included two pairs of shorts and two short sleeve blouses, with a straw hat thrown in. It appears that Marla was planning a trip. As soon as she got in the house, she headed straight for the shower, had lunch with her mother, and dad was at work. He doesn't get home until after 5:30 PM, unless he has a piece of property to show and the employees have left the office. Mr. Fletcher has one rule of thumb and that is he never allows a woman to show a piece of property after dark unless she's accompanied by a male. There were a couple of instances where a lady had to fight off what she believed to be a client. The man was after more than a piece of property. After dinner, and some small talk. Marla begins to pack her clothes. The weekend was only a day away and she had plenty to do.

Mr. Fletcher helped her load the tent along with some tools, like an ax for cutting wood for the fire. He found the small barbecue grill still buried under a pile of paper and boxes. "Are you having the barbecue Marla?"

"No dad, we decided to take this heavy flat grill we're going to lay across the rocks over the fireplace and use it instead of the grill."

"Well, sweetheart, I see you've got your thinking hat on. I knew you were smart; you surprise me more every day." He said lovingly. He was very happy with his daughter. "Oh, sweetheart. I left the flashlight in the den, mind getting it for me? I think I left it on the desk."

"Sure dad, not a problem." She turned and walked away, entering the house through the garage door leading into the kitchen, then she reached the den. The flashlight was right where he said it would be. When she returned to the garage. Her father was talking to himself, "what's up pops you turn into a soliloquist?" She questioned with laughter.

"Well, sometimes when there's nobody else to talk to. However, I haven't started answering yet." He replied with a smile.

After dinner, Marla told her parents she was going to the diner and have a conversation with Brenda about the trip, she should be there by 8:30."

Marla arrived at the diner. 8:25 PM Brenda had yet to show up. However, she didn't get off work until eight. Unless of course there was an emergency.

Shortly after seated in the booth. Brenda comes bounding through the rear door panting as though she just ran a marathon.

"Well," Marla said, "where have you been, I've been here for 30 minutes?" (That was a lie.)

Brenda came back with, "some of us have to work for a living and that wouldn't be you." She wasn't truthful, Marla only stayed at home because she enjoyed being with her family. She could afford to rent but why, at least this way she had plenty of company.

Brenda answered, "I was just kidding. After all, I have a home too." Well, I've got about 15 minutes before I have to get behind the bar, so what are you going to do?

"I think I'll have one of those braless Maggie's." She said, making the mistake of using the word bra instead of salt.

Brenda broke into laughter. After explaining the error, they both had a good laugh. "Brenda, I have to go in tomorrow for a few hours, but I'll be back home by noon. Are you ready to start packing your stuff in the car? I guess we should head out the next morning. We'll swing by the Market on the way out of town and pick up the food and pack it in the cooler and then we're out of here. Have you made all the arrangements with Frank?"

"Oh yeah, everything is set to go and I'm getting anxious to get out of Dodge." Brenda replied.

Friday finally came, the girls were locked and loaded. The only thing left was a shortstop at the supermarket.

CHAPTER 3

A LITTLE VACATION

Friday morning at 8:00 AM sharp, Marla said goodbye to her parents, climbed behind the wheel of her dad's SUV and drove off to pick up Brenda. It wouldn't take her long, Brenda only lived 3 miles from the Fletcher's. She arrived in about five minutes give or take a minute. When she arrived at Brenda's house she went inside, said hello and goodbye to the Patterson's, Brenda's parents.

Brenda was in the kitchen drinking a cup of coffee, "Would you care for a cup, Marla?" she asked.

"Sure, I'm positive we have plenty of time." She returned.

Brenda's father was at work, her mother was in the kitchen sitting next to Brenda.

Brenda's mother spoke "hi sweetie," she said, addressing Marla who walked over to where Mrs. Patterson was sitting and gave her a hug. "How are you doing this morning mom?" They were very close, but then they had known each other since the girls were 11 years old, and in the fifth grade.

"Well, Brenda, I guess we better hit the road, we have a long drive ahead of us and it would be nice to get in early enough to pitch the tent and build a fire pit before dark."

"Okay Marla, I'll just rinse out the cups and we're out of here."

"Don't worry about 2 cups. I'm sure I can handle them, you girls better get on the road, but be careful. You never know what you might run into up there in the forest." Mrs. Patterson warned.

The two left the house and headed for the supermarket to buy the necessities to survive in the almost wilderness. They left the city and drove about 30 miles over seemingly flat ground. It was a little up and down. They reached a point where the road was starting to climb up a long winding road necessary to reach their destination.

After traveling for nearly 3 hours, Brenda had a need to relieve her bladder. There was a rest area about 5 miles further up the road, she was twisting and turning as if it was life-threatening. And then she crossed her legs and squeezed tight, "hurry up Marla or I'm going to let go of your seat." She must've really been miserable.

"You had better not," Marla warned, "this is my dad's car and his pride and joy. I don't think he would appreciate your leaking on the seats."

"Leaking hell, if I don't let go pretty soon, I'll flood the whole front of the car," Brenda threatened.

Marla had a similar problem, but apparently not as severe as Brenda's. She pulled into the rest area parking lot parking as close to the bathroom as she could get. Brenda was out of the car before it came to a stop. Must've been embarrassing watching her trying to run with both hands over pelvis, do you suppose people could figure out what the problem was?

The placating was over. Brenda had to go before she had already gone.

Marla got out of the car, as calm as could be. Of course, it was just for show, as soon as she entered the bathroom, she made a mad dash for the nearest stall. There was no one available. Now it was her turn to do the Indian war dance.

Marla fought her way into the stall that Brenda was exiting. She had a refreshing look on her face. Shortly, Marla came out, they both went to the sink and washed up well, climbed back in the car and were underway, it would be another hour before they reached your destination.

The mountain slope gradually inclined as the girls proceeded towards the area where they planned to settle in for the night. To make matters worse it began to drizzle, not a lot of heavy rain just enough to make it miserable.

Fortunately, they didn't have to go to the bathroom again because there wouldn't be another one for several miles beyond the turnoff they would be taking to the campsite.

After an hour, give or take, they came to a fork in the road and they took a right turn. They would only be going another three or 4 miles, they could hardly wait.

Finally, they reached an area that was somewhat secluded and off of the road a couple hundred feet towards the lake.

Marla spotted a place; it was pretty level with a couple pine trees and a large oak tree. It looked like an excellent place to build a fire pit and set the tent up. That way if it did rain the oak tree would stop some of the rainwater from hitting the tent.

She backed the car up alongside the oak tree. They climbed down out of the car and started pitching the tent," Brenda, go ahead and start finding the rocks to build your fireplace while I get started on the tent, as soon as I finish, I'll help you. I also have to gather enough wood to get us through the night.

It was getting dark out. The only light they had was that from the fire. They were warm and comfortable, for now.

Marla asked "what do you think we should have for dinner Brenda, it's not like we have a big choice, but I'm sure we can find something in the ice chest we can eat.

"Well," Brenda said, "I know one thing, it won't be fresh trout, and there's no guarantee we will have it tomorrow night either, you know, fish don't just jump on the hook."

"I guess," Marla said, "we'll have to figure that out when it's daylight. Finally, about 11 o'clock that night they decided it was time to go to bed.

They both climbed into the tent, covered up and immediately went to sleep until one of them started snoring, the other punched her in the ribs. "Stop snoring Brenda, you're keeping me awake."

"I can't help it, I'm just tired. When you are tired you snore, aren't you tired at all?" Brenda questioned.

"No," Marla said, "and I'm too tired to snore. Besides, I'd rather sleep. So, go back to sleep but do it quietly. We have to get up early in the morning if we're to catch any fish. Dad says they bite best early in the morning and late in the evening so what's your pleasure?"

Brenda said, "Let's draw straws to see whether it's morning or evening, right now I prefer the evening."

"Whenever this chilly weather warms up so we can get out of bed." Marla said.

Finally, they fell asleep, somehow the snoring no longer bothered Marla.

She just chimed in with Brenda until the morning came.

Marla was the first to rise. The next morning she walked over to the Lake, bent down and washed her face and hands, drying them on the towel she took from the car. It was coffee time. First there had to be a fire. She stuck her head inside the tent and started shaking Brenda's feet. Brenda was startled and jumped to her feet, "what's going on." She queried.

"I need help, Marla said we've got to get together and build a fire so we can have coffee this morning, I can't do it all by myself so get your butt out of there and give me a hand."

Brenda crawled out of the tent, stretching and yawning, asking, "what time is it?"

Marla returned with, "daytime, time rise and shine. I'm hungry and we have no fire. Help me gather some wood and get the fire started and I'll bring out the skillet and have some bacon and eggs; how does that sound?"

The two girls worked together and soon there was a fire blazing.

Marla got the 10-inch skillet from the car and the bacon from the ice chest while Brenda was still gathering more wood. They used the screen that was laid over the firepit and across resting on the surrounding rocks. "Should we attempt to toast on the screen, Brenda?" Marla asked.

"Might as well, just be sure and keep an eye on it. I'll burn faster than a toaster."

Soon breakfast was over, it was time to go fishing, "we'll clean the pan when we get back." Said Marla. Fortunately, they had bought paper plates so there will be no dish washing.

Brenda climbed into the rear of the SUV and pulled out the fishing gear, two rods and reels plus a tackle box containing hooks and sinkers. They made their way to the lake to find a comfortable spot where they could sit while waiting for the fish to bite.

Down the bank of the lake about 200 feet, there was a boat landing that extended over the water and out about 50 to 60 feet, "what do you think Marla, should we try our luck from the landing?"

"Sounds like a plan to me," she replied, "at least it beats sitting on the dirty ground."

They strolled down the bank to where the dock was and entered the walkway. There was a ladder descending to the water, "I guess if we don't catch any fish, we can always go swimming." Brenda suggested.

"Don't be so negative, we haven't even cast lines out yet." Marla returned.

They sat in the sun at the end of the landing with their feet dangling over the side. They put some fish eggs on their hooks and cast them in the water and waited patiently for a bite. As long as they've known each other they still had plenty to talk about, reminiscing about the past few years and where their life was going. It seemed both were happy with their lives.

"Brenda, do you think we will ever find a good-looking man to date? It's been a long time, and I've found myself feeling a bit lonely, the present company excluded. But then there's a gender gap there isn't there? I'm not that way. Ha Ha.

"Yeah. I've felt that way too, I guess we haven't been trying, we're kind of waiting for someone to come along and sweep us off our feet, are we that ugly that we can't find one on our own?" Brenda asked.

"Well for the time being let's just concentrate on catching some fish for dinner. Who knows there just might be someone out here that will come along and say, "what are you two gorgeous ladies doing out here in the wilderness when you should be on a pedestal?" Marla said being funny.

"Yeah, fat chance, by coming up here where God only knows what the odds are?"

Shortly after the question came up two nice looking gentlemen approached the girls, "do you mind if we join you, we haven't had any luck where we were fishing, maybe you can bring us some luck."

The girls looked at each other bewildered thinking what do we have to lose? How is it possible after just talking about two nice gentlemen showing up, yet here they are, why let an opportunity like this slip away?

"Sure, find a space and cast your spell on us, we're not having much luck either, perhaps we can bring luck for all." Marla said.

The two cowboy-looking gentlemen took a seat next to the girls one on each side as though they were meant to be paired. "By the way, my name is Jack and my friend over there is Fred, and if you don't mind telling us your name, we won't have to say 'hey you' every time we ask a question."

Marla looked at Brenda. She looked back. One of them raised her eyebrow indicating "why not?" "My name is Marla, and my friend's name is Brenda we're from Pleasantville and we're both nurses and we're just here for the weekend."

"Well that's nice, it's a pleasure to meet you ladies." said the bowlegged cowboy.

During the introduction Marla pulled her line in to check and see if there was anything on it.

Jack noticed that she had a fish egg on the hook; he made a comment, "Is that what you've been using all this time? Here, let me put a worm on the hook for you and see if you have better luck. They don't seem to bite those eggs. I don't know why sometimes they're better than worms and sometimes they're not."

He put the worm on her hook and told her to cast out as far as she could and then reel it in slowly, "it works for me when the fish are biting."

Marla cast out with all her might landing the hook about thirty feet. She let it hit bottom then started slowly began reeling it in just as Jack told her, and lo and behold the line began to jerk. Just a little at first, until Jack said, "jerk back on the pole you have to set the hook."

She did what was directed and soon she was pulling a pretty nice size fish.

This excited everyone and they all began to bait up and get their lines in the water. Soon they had seven fish, all nice sizes.

"Well," said Marla, "since you showed us the way, you're invited to join us for dinner, that is what you want to do."

There was little doubt to what their answer was, "well, thank you ma'am, speaking for both of us, I'd say we would be delighted." (I just bet they would.)

They all gathered around the campfire and told stories, mostly getting acquainted, (and a lot of lies.)

After dinner they sat and talked, after all, there wasn't anyone else around, and it appeared the girls were enjoying themselves, they hadn't talked to many males in a long time, except for the doctors and some nurses.

They talked until after midnight until Marla said, "I think it's past our bedtime Brenda, and I'm getting sleepy." She told the men that they really enjoyed their company, "maybe we can do it again tomorrow, we're leaving Monday morning."

They all agreed to meet again tomorrow, everyone said goodnight and they parted ways, (temporarily.)

The girls laid in bed and talked for hours, mostly about the newfound male friends and what to do with them. "I wonder if they live in Pleasantville," Brenda asked.

"I don't know but I will be sure to find out. They are both very handsome and polite as well. Do you suppose they're always slick, or perhaps they have their moments as well? Wouldn't it be great if they invited us and they had steak?"

"Yeah, but I wouldn't count on it. Maybe we could combine what we have with theirs. But what do we have to offer?"

"Don't see anything like that in front of them. They both begin to laugh loudly. We better get some sleep, or we'll be in bed until noon."

The two finally fell asleep. Soon, the night was gone. The next morning, after building a fire and having coffee, they each had a piece of coffeecake, cleaned up the mess and decided whether to go fishing or not.

Marla said, "let's go where we were yesterday only this time, we'll wear our bathing suits under our clothes in case we decide to go swimming. It might be dangerous out there, if the water is too cold maybe we can just tease them a little."

Brenda said, "let's take our poles to see if the fish are biting. Who knows we may get lucky?"

"Don't ever say that again, you know what I mean, Silly." Marla scolded with the touch of laughter.

They entered the landing and to their surprise; the guys were there sitting at the end of the dock fishing poles in her hand.

"Good morning gentlemen, did you sleep well?" Brenda asked.

"Oh yes ma'am, like a log you two must've slept well. It's almost 1 o'clock." Fred and I have been here since 7:30 AM. Look, we caught four nice size fish, you two up for dinner again tonight?"

Yeah Marla said, "but we were hoping for something other than fish like a nice sizzling steak."

"Well" said Jack, "we could go into town, have a steak and be back in about six hours." He was kind of joking, I think.

"You are not serious, are you? I don't think we're interested in spending all night, even for a steak!" Brenda returned.

"Well," Jack said, "I was serious but I'm glad you decided not to go. Maybe we might have a couple of pork chops if you like pork."

"Brenda said. "I'm not crazy about pork, we have two small steaks if you want to put them together hell, you might even throw in a couple of fish."

"Sounds good to me," Jack said, speaking for both of them.

They mixed up a decent dinner and lots of conversation. It was finally 11 o'clock and surprisingly Jack spoke up saying, "we have to cut it short tonight, Fred and I are leaving early in the morning, don't want to drive in that heavy traffic."

"Oh, it should be all that bad. There doesn't seem to be very many people here, at least not much of a crowd."

"Well, Fred and I work on a ranch about 30 miles east of Pleasantville and we need to get home early enough to check out the stock before nightfall."

"Okay, Jack, whatever you say, Brenda and I enjoyed your company. Perhaps we can meet again sometime." Marla said.

"Well, you know," Jack said, "If we had your phone numbers, I can guarantee it."

All four exchanged phone numbers and it looked like there'd be a party down the road sometime. The girls are going to have to learn cowboy talk.

Brenda spoke, "I work at Frank's bar and grill almost every night. I'm usually behind the bar until closing time. But sometimes, I have to work the diner. If Marla is available, she will be there as well. It all depends on her shift at the hospital."

Everyone agreed, they even shook hands and said goodbye and the cowboy walked away, waving their hands.

Marla said after the Cowboys left and were out of sight. "I hope we didn't set ourselves up for heartache."

"Calm down," Brenda said, "we haven't even had a date. Besides, it just might turn out to be okay."

Memorial Day weekend, it was nearing time for the girls to head for home. They slept in till 11 o'clock, cooked their last breakfast on their holiday weekend trip. After they finally finished eating, they cleaned up and began to pack the vehicle for the long journey home.

Marla said, "since we haven't gone swimming, we might as well this morning, take a bar soap maybe we can take a partial bath at least."

"sounds like a plan to me. Let's finish loading up the car and hit the drink." Brenda agreed.

By 3:30, they were packed, bathed and ready to go. Marla said, "you know I miss my hiking, what you say we lock the vehicle and take a short hike up the mountainside?"

"Well," Brenda said, "since you're driving, I guess you'd be the boss. So, let's hit the trail."

There were no trails marked by John Muir, so they had to blaze their own. They started climbing and zigzagging through the trees, and like Hansel and Gretel they marked some of the trees, making sure not to get lost on their way back.

They hiked and hiked for 10 or 15 minutes then stopped to rest for a few minutes and then back to hiking. Brenda was following Marla's lead.

Approximately 200 yards up the mountainside. Marla put her hand behind her so Brenda couldn't pass, "Do you smell that Brenda? it smells like decay, probably a dead animal." She declared.

They proceeded to climb when suddenly Marla stopped in her tracks. "Look, Brenda, she pulled her head to the side of Marla so she could see," "What is that?" she asked.

"Marla, let's not go any closer, it looks like a body. We should stay back, engulf everything we can." Brenda was standing about 10 feet away from the body. She said, "It's a woman who's wearing a brown skirt with a yellow blouse."

"What else should we do and why are we playing detective?"

"Because," Marla explained, "when we got back, the rest area, I'm sure I saw a payphone there. We need to call the police department and make them aware of our discovery. So, every little thing we see we have to tell like them, and the beer can by her feet, and the color of her clothes. The more we tell them the better chance we have not to have to return to point out the body."

Brenda said, "you're not going to like my suggestion, but start tearing so many pieces of your new blouse, and hang them on the trees that we marked coming up the trail so they can find their way back."

"Are you nuts? I paid 20 bucks for this blouse. You tear some of your old blouse that you're wearing." The suggestion didn't go well with Brenda. However, she began to strip her blouse in pieces, as they passed their markers. She would tie a small piece of her blouse onto the tree, hoping they wouldn't have to return.

They finally made it back to the car, they climbed into their seats and sat there for a few minutes processing all they had witnessed.

They were still talking about the discovery two hours later when they pulled into the rest stop.

Marla parked the car as close to the phone booth that she could get, "you might as well go to the bathroom while we're here, not stopping again." She said in a demanding voice.

Marla called 911. The operator asked her what her emergency was. She explained about the body discovery in detail. After hearing what Marla had to say the operator sent her call directly to the Police Department.

The Police Department where the call was directed knew it was out of their jurisdiction, but of course Marla could not have known that. Hello Sgt. Bradford, answered. "How can I help you?"

"Well, I think I can help you. You know where Pine flats are?"

"Yes, I do but it's out of our jurisdiction, that would be the sheriff department in that area. I'll tell you what, just give me the information. I'll make the call."

Marla described in detail all that she and Brenda had witnessed. She even told Sgt. about leaving markers and how to find the body as well as to let them know to start from the backside of the big oak tree. She said my name is Marla Fletcher and I'm a nurse and I work at the Memorial Hospital. If you need me to go in and make a statement. My number is," she proceeded to give them the number where she lived, where she worked. She supplied the Sgt. with all her personal information and said "anything else I can help you with give me a call."

The Sgt. thanked her and said, "I'll call you if I need anything else. Thank you for the information." After which he hung up the phone.

It so happened there was a small town just 30 miles north of Pine Flats Road. It also had a Sheriff's station. The Sgt. called the sheriff and gave him all the details to start the search.

Sheriff Barr said he would get on it immediately. Before hanging up the phone Sgt. asked, "Mr. Barr, Please let me know your discovery may be connected to a bank robbery that occurred just recently in fact, less than a week ago."

The sheriff promised he would let them know as soon as he found the body. At that, he hung up the phone.

The Sgt. went down the hall to Sgt. Baker's office, "Ed, I think we might have found the body of the woman that was kidnapped during the robbery last week. I've got Sheriff Barr on it as we speak. It seems these two ladies went camping at Pine Flats and while hiking up the side of the mountain they discovered a body, the body that may well match the same person that was kidnapped. She was wearing the same clothes as the victim, and it was exactly what the body was wearing."

"Did you get the name of the woman that gave you all this information?" Sgt. Baker asked.

"Absolutely, she not only gave me her name but her phone number where she worked as well as her home address."

"Okay, let's search the file and see what we can dig up, we might as well start questioning the people again. Maybe this time they'll remember something different that they didn't know at the time we interviewed them."

Sgt. Baker and his partner went from one witness to the other, asking the same questions, hoping now the witnesses had something more to add.

They knocked on the first door, a lady answered. The Sgt. showed his badge and was invited into the house. The questioning began, "ma'am, we were hoping you might've remembered something else about the men that robbed the bank and any little thing you might remember would be greatly appreciated."

"No, sir, the ladies said only what I told you before, actually, I've been trying hard not to think about it. It's not an experience I'll soon forget."

The officers thanked the lady and headed towards the door.

"Oh," said the informant, "there is one small thing. You may already know, but I noticed that one of the robbers was tall, the other one was short. The tall one had the lady in front of him as they backed out the door. He held the gun to this lady's head and when they got out the door, I could see through his mask that his eyes were blue. He was apparently wearing the mask separate from the hood. I know he was very angry with his partner for allowing the door to hit the mask where it stuck out the most. Anyway, he's got blue eyes if that'll help."

"Well," said Sgt. Baker, "It may seem like something very small but is actually great to know we're looking for a blue-eyed man, thank you very much for your cooperation."

They left and drove away to the next witnesses residence. "You know if all the witnesses have another little clue and maybe will be able to find a match after all."

"So now, we have a red van and a blue-eyed bandit kidnapper and possibly a killer. Wouldn't it be great if the drugstore bandit kid killer/ bank robbery and murder were all one and the same?" Baker said with a sarcastic tone.

"Fat chance" he said, "crimes are never that simple to solve. But it would kill several birds with one bullet."

"Yeah, you are right about that. However, crimes like this are seldom simple, we'll have to wait until the sheriff homicide division finally launches their investigation. Even then, they may not come up with any usable evidence. Perhaps they can lift some fingerprints from the beer can, that's what her name is, oh yeah, Marla Fletcher, if it works out and the prints from the can matches the ones, we have on file from the fingerprints we lifted from the car involved in the drugstore and hit-and-run. I guess that's the only way to know if it's all one and the same."

"Well Ed until that happens, I guess we will have to sit on our duff and wait."

"I don't think so, we have to keep digging, I mean why should it be so hard to find a red Ford van, I mean how many could there be in this town. Let's keep it under wraps but notify everyone on the force. Even the sheriff department keeps an eye out for the red Ford van. Maybe they can get the license number. We can run it through the DMV and find out who the owner is, probably stolen, but we can hope." Said the Sgt. "Besides, with the end of the road unless we get a gigantic break."

Marla was home but still struggling with the discovery of the body, oh she saw many bodies in the hospital but never one immersion in the weeds. She was just trying to cope.

Brenda, on the other hand, was doing much. I don't know why I doubt she had ever witnessed a scene like that before. Yet she didn't let it get to her. Brenda will find a way to comfort Marla, they have a lot of camaraderie between them. But then they've been together most of their lives.

CHAPTER 4

HI HO SILVER

A week went by, Marla appeared to be improving, of course, she wouldn't let the event keep her from her nursing skills. Her patients needed all of her skills and attention.

Brenda's shift at the hospital went into the PM, but her day's work was far from over. It was time to take over Frank's bar and grill and at least relieve the bartender.

She was delightfully surprised when she arrived at work to find Fred and Jack sitting at the bar having a beer.

"Well," she said, somewhat startled by their appearance, "hi guys, what brings you to town and how's the cow business?" She said facetiously.

Jack spoke, "where's Marla we were hoping to see both of you at the same time?"

"Well, let's see, I think she worked the midnight shift which means she's probably home, give me a minute I'll call and see if she can come over for a drink, she should be up and around by now."

Brenda, after excusing herself, went to the phone and dialed Marla's number. Marla's dad answered the phone, "Hello this is Ted, how can I help you?" That's kind of the way he would answer the phone at work thinking it was a client. "Is your lovely daughter handy?" Brenda asked.

"Well hello sweetie," Mr. Fletcher said he knew who it was as soon as he answered the phone, "hold on, I'll get her for you."

"Thanks, pop," were her only words.

Marla answered the phone, "what's up Brenda? you have a problem for me to solve?" She chuckled.

"Yeah, sort of I've got a pair of cowboys sitting here in front of me. One of them is seeking your company. Can you come over for a drink or two and a little conversation?" Brenda queried.

"Sure, I think I can accommodate you, for a little while anyway I have the midnight shift again tonight."

"Well, you only have to stay as long as you want, I'm sure the cowboys will understand. I imagine they will have to get back to the ranch sometime this evening."

Marla dressed up slick. Nothing like making a great impression. You never know what might develop. When she walked into the bar all eyes were on Marla. She was truly beautiful, but then she looked beautiful wearing burlap.

"Hi guys, what's going on? We haven't seen you in weeks, well, almost a week. Did Brenda tell you what happened to us after you left Pine flats?"

"Yeah," Jack said, "I bet that was frightening."

"It was more than just frightening, it was horrifying. We couldn't get out of there fast enough. However, we had the presence of mine to make a mental note of what the victim was wearing and other clues that were around the immediate area. So, when we notified the police, they would have some idea what to expect when they arrived."

"You two ladies sure are brave, I hate to make either of you mad. I might end up in the hospital and you're looking down on me." Jack said jokingly.

"It's not that we're brave, we've just seen death in many forms, this was just a different situation than in the hospital."

The tale of victims' bodies and death turned to another subject, one much more appealing like horseback riding.

Jack asked the question, "do you ladies like to ride horses?"

Marla said, "I used to enjoy riding a lot when I was younger, but I haven't been on a horse since I was in grade school, but I remember it was really fun."

"What about you Brenda, do you ride?"

"I think the last time I was with Marla so, that was also in grammar school. I would like to try again sometime If I were invited." Brenda answered.

"Oh, Brenda," Marla said, "you're embarrassing, why don't you just say what you mean and quit hinting around the bush?"

"Well, I was just making a statement!" She said extending the opportunity to be asked.

"Why don't you just invite yourself, I'm sure old Fred there would be most accommodating." Marla said being facetious.

Fred jumped into the conversation," you're invited any time you want, you too Marla. We would be more than happy to have you on the ranch for a day and see how we live."

"I guess in that case," Marla said, "we should set a time it's available for all. It would work best on the weekend, she said. Brenda and I are usually off on weekends."

"That's great," Jack said, "we usually finish by 5 o'clock on weekends. So, since it's still light till after seven, there will be plenty of daylight for a ride. Because we're not planning the ranch trip for two weeks, how about a movie next Saturday night."

Marla looked at Brenda, who returned to look, her eyebrow raised. Said "great," "there's a movie at the Fox theater I've been wanting to see. I can't remember the name but it's sort of romantic, yet diabolical as well." "It should be interesting."

"Great idea, Brenda I've been wanting to go to the movies for a long time now with everybody's approval we finally get to go." Marla said with determination.

The week went by fast; it was Saturday before you could say chicken cricket. However, on Wednesday, Brenda quit her job at Frank's, she no longer needed to work two jobs. She was still living at her parents' house and paying a small amount of rent so she wouldn't feel like a leech, although her parents would never have felt that way, she was after all, the only child in the family.

Marla was surprised that Brenda quit her job. She was a good bartender. I'm sure she will be missed by Frank.

They both pulled the same shift on Friday, making it easy to be together on Saturday for the date. They've been waiting for to the ranch, however, that was another week away. This was Saturday, coming up for the movie.

Jack opened the door on the passenger side and assisted Marla into the car. Fred followed suit, and they drove off for a night downtown to the Fox theater to see this movie they've been waiting to see.

They went inside, handed the usher the tickets and were shown where their seats were located.

"Popcorn anyone?" Jack asks. And he brought two boxes of popcorn one for Brenda and Fred and the other for Marla and himself. The girls also had a soft drink, the guys declined, I believe they were waiting for thereafter movie beer.

There was an exciting moment during the romantic scene. Marla covered her mouth with her hands as though she was about to cry and didn't want anybody else to see. A perfect moment for Jack to put his arm around Marla and with no resistance. However, I doubt she even noticed.

Jack was careful that he didn't make a move on Marla. He thought perhaps there might be another moment of sudden fear and then the move would be as if he was comforting her. I'm sure there will be more moments after all, it was a diabolically/romantic movie and there's usually several jumping, frightening scenes. There were some very romantic scenes while Marla would tear up, she even during one tear jerking scene laid her head back on Jack's shoulder. He put his arm around her back and his hand on her shoulder pulling her closer to him, she still didn't get it, or she embraced it.

The week passed and it was another Saturday, Marla got a call from Jack asking, "do you want us to pick you up at home or should we meet at Franks and have a drink before we go back to the ranch?"

"Sure," she said, "I'll pick up Brenda and meet at Frank's place. We can never leave wondering what might happen while trekking down the highway."

"That's great, Fred and I will meet you there at Frank's at 7 PM. Then we can all go together but I guess that will work probably better if you drive since you're returning the same night," Jack said, "we'll see you there at seven sugar."

"Oh, oh," she thought, "I believe that was a term of endearment. I wonder what's next? Maybe I'm just over protecting myself it's been so long since I've been on a date. I'm not sure how to act. I guess I'll just have to let the chips fall where they may.'

Marla went home and talked to her family, they knew she hadn't dated for a while. "Well, mom and dad, Brenda and I met these two gentlemen while on vacation. They asked us out to the movies last Saturday and we accepted, of course, that was a week ago this Saturday, were invited to visit them on the ranch and were going to go horseback riding."

"Well," said Mr. Fletcher, "will we meet them when they come to pick you up?"

"No, dad, not this time we're meeting them at Frank's, but I'll see to it you meet them on Saturday before we go to the ranch. I'm going to pick up Brenda so they can meet her folks then and then I'll bring them over here so you can say hello. I think you're gonna like them, they're very nice people."

(Dad is still protective of me after all these years, of course, at 26 I'm still his little girl.)

Marla called Brenda seeking an answer on how the guys could meet their parents and hopefully ease their minds.

Brenda responded with, "the only way I can think of is if we can find a way for them to pick us up at home, we'll talk it over with them when they arrive."

I know Marla said, "if they stay overnight or come back on Sunday. We can let them meet our families and maybe go to the park on Sunday and have a picnic before they return to the ranch, how does that sound?"

The two were pulling the same shift, "well Marla, tomorrow is the big day. Are you ready to straddle a horse?" She asked facetiously. Brenda continued to say to Marla, "since you are driving tomorrow why don't you come by early enough for breakfast? I'm sure mom and dad would love to see you?"

"Sounds good to me. I'd love to see your folks again. It's been a long time since a bit over the maybe they won't even recognize me "she said jokingly.

"Don't be silly, there's no way they could forget your face. It's been around for too many years and I'm sure we will have a great get together, So, plan on it, Okay?"

"Don't worry about me, Brenda, I'll be there with my riding boots on. Which reminds me, I don't have any. How do you ride a horse without riding boots?" She was laughing all the way through the sentence.

Brenda said, "nobody could ever forget you, just be sure to be on the horse alone. Don't let Jack talk you into riding sidesaddle. I wonder what that's like. I've never tried riding a sidesaddle. It seemed like I could slip off the edge and hit the ground running, now that's being silly, we both know how to ride a horse."

"Okay partner, I'll see you in the morning, have breakfast and head for the ranch."

Marla was up, showered and ready to go by 8:30. Her mom asked her where she was going in such a hurry.

"Remember mom, I told you Brenda and I were going horseback riding today?"

"Well yes dear, I remember your telling me and your dad. Be sure and take the proper wear for horseback riding."

"Well mom, if you remember the rest of the story, I said I was dining with Brenda at her house today with her and her parents, that is."

"Oh, that's right, be sure and tell them I said hello."

"Okay mom, I'll see to it so she knows you're thinking about her."

Marla left home at 8:45 AM and headed towards Patterson's, she arrived at the 9 o'clock course. It was only 3 miles."

She rang the doorbell, Brenda's mother answered, "come give me a hug. Marla had to be careful not to squeeze her too tight. She was five foot eight and weighed about 145 pounds," where Brenda's mom, is only five foot one weighs 100 – pounds wringing wet.

They had a huge breakfast, they never knew when they might eat again, so they had a big one. She was wondering who did the cooking on the ranch. I guess they would know how by now.

Marla drove for about 40 minutes watching closely for a sign marked circle J. They didn't know what it meant but were pretty sure it wasn't for Jack. Jack rode up to the gate to let the girls in. Marla and Brenda entered while Jack secured the gate behind them, "Park over yonder by the house." She followed Jack's instructions. Then she and Marla climbed out of the car with Fred closed behind. He helped her out of the vehicle saying, "let's go into the house and I'll show you around. He helped Marla up the steps, "be careful. Come all the way up to the house and be careful not to stumble, or fall, you would want to mess up that beautiful face." Jack said, "we didn't have you come all the way out here to stumble and fall."

Marla asked, a little doubtful about walking into a strange house with two guys that they only met for a few weeks ago while they were on their Memorial Day weekend.

Brenda asked, "the owners, where are they?"

"Their away leaving us in charge they'll be back on Monday we been watching the place for them for almost 7 years, I guess they figure after all that time, they could trust us"

"Well, it kind of sounds like it," the girls thought, 'we didn't come all the way out here to chicken out now.'

Jack said, "come on and I'll give you the grand tour."

They follow Jack through one room and into another. "Like many ranch houses they're made of knotty pine, it looks good if you keep it clean." Jack commented.

After seeing the entire house and making many comments. Fred asked, "would you ladies like something to drink?"

"It's a little early don't you think?" Brenda commented, not realizing they were talking about water, soda, anything other than alcohol.

"Ma'am, I meant soda or water, not Alcohol. I'm sorry if I gave you the wrong impression."

"It's okay Fred, I was only joking anyway." She said apologetically.

All four left the residence and went outside where the cowboys slept. There was a bunkhouse just 40 feet from the barn. It was surprisingly clean. Of course, there was, not a kitchen, but a bunkhouse with two beds and a bathroom. Containing a shower, toilet and all the good things needed for a bathroom. The men explained that they eat at the same time every night. And the reason for that regimen was because the lady of the house had breakfast on the table at 7:30 AM sharp. Now should you happen to sleep in beyond that time, you would have to skip breakfast and wait for lunch."

Of course, cowboys aren't stupid. They keep some food in the bunkhouse. However, they were allowed to use the kitchen when the owners were away.

Next to the bunkhouse was the barn and like everything else on the ranch it was kept very clean. The bales of hay were stacked neatly, and the piles of loose hay tended to droop and fall onto the ground no matter who piled it.

The stables were also clean as you could clean them under the circumstances. It was close to noon when Fred said, "would you like to have lunch before we go riding?"

"No, Marla said looking at Brenda explaining the two had a late breakfast like 9 o'clock, I'm sure we can wait until after the ride, depending on how long the ride lasts."

I guess that our next step would be to select the horses we're going to ride. "Marla, you want a tame horse that you can ride, or do you think you can handle one that's a little wilder? Just pick any horse and I'll saddled up"

Marla said, "I like this one, is it tame? I haven't ridden for a long time and I would prefer not to get bucked off on my first ride."

The guys picked two horses that were tame and gentle enough for the girls to ride. They helped the ladies mount the horses and soon they were off on a trip they will long remember.

"Where are we heading Jack?" Marla asked, wondering if they plan to take them to a desolate place that only they knew was an attempt to take advantage of them.

The ranch was located at the bottom of a mountain with plenty of trees. Marla thought, 'I was hoping I would never be carried into the woods again after what we went through a few weeks ago.'

The word trail took them into the words that the trail was only wide enough for one horse at a time without hitting a tree.

They rode for about an hour. Jack led the party, followed by Marla with Brenda close behind, Fred brought up the rear.

They came to a large flat circular area at the crest of the trail. Jack said, "would you like to stop and rest for a while?"

Marla spoke, "yeah, it looks like you can see forever from this vantage point let's get down and walk around we to walk off these bowlegs."

Jack helped Marla offer horses as did Fred with Brenda. "It's beautiful here, no trees to block your view and like Marla said, you can see forever. Too bad we didn't pack lunch. We could've had a picnic.

They wandered around, stopping every now and again to take a look in the view of the valley below. They were up about 3000 feet giving a great view of the valley below.

Brenda was complaining about how her legs felt from straddling the saddle.

"Well," said Fred, "which do you prefer, the straddle or side saddle, might settle your legs, however, they may be scorer in other places.

"No thanks, I'll survive." Brenda commented.

They walked over to the side of the clearing. Jack said, "Do you see that large boulder over yonder, that's a marker for the property and it extends towards where we're standing and a few hundred feet over yonder." He said as he pointed in the direction of the property border.

"Wow, Marta said in disbelief. All that area down below and up two or 300 feet behind us. That's one heck of a piece of property."

"You bet your life," Jack said, 420 acres. "That's a lot more property than we need. Of course, we grow our own alfalfa, so they don't have to pay for hay for the horses and the 40 cows. We also have about 50 hens that are supplied with eggs. We also sell plenty of chickens to people that don't want to be bothered taking care of them, especially cleaning up after them. Yeah, we have plenty to keep us busy, hang around after dinner and you can see how we operate."

"What do you mean dinner, are you telling us, you're also the cooks? We missed lunch somewhere along the way."

"We'll take care of that issue as soon as we get down off the mountain." Fred said it like a vow.

Well, Jack said, "let's saddle up and head down to lunch. What do you say guys?"

They climbed back in the saddle and off they went headed down the slope towards the ranch house, it was lunch time.

After they reached the bottom of the hill they dismounted near the stable. Fred and Jack began to pull the saddles off the horses. Then the blankets and the bridles, swatted the horses on the rump and they found their way back into the stables.

Meanwhile, Marla and Brenda slowly walked towards the ranch house wondering who was preparing lunch. To their surprise when they were all four together. Jack pulled a tray from the refrigerator with stacks of luncheon meat, cheese, lettuce, tomato, mayonnaise and a few other condiments. He put them on the table and said, "ladies help yourself while I pour the wine."

"Well Jack, it looks like you thought of everything, good job." Everyone raised their glasses and said, "Here's to Jack, May he always be our host." They left after lunch after a four hour drive to the fields and pastures. "Very impressive," the girls both agreed.

Jack gave each girl a basket, "what are we supposed to do with these?" Brenda asked."

"I'm about to show you, watch me and then do as I do and don't chicken out, a little poultry humor there." He started gathering eggs and putting them into the basket.

The girls thought no problem. So, they selected a nest and began gathering eggs.

"So, this is how it works, I always thought they came in Styrofoam boxes." The guys began to laugh, "this is just the first step. They go from here to different companies where they are put on a special belt to be washed, dried and then packed into a variety of containers like cardboard and Styrofoam packages. So, you see when you get them at the store you will appreciate them all the more, and how much that egg is worth before it gets to your table."

The girls applauded Jack's explanation of the process of the eggs. He bowed before the girls, putting one arm across his chest and he continued his story, "the chickens are also sold to poultry companies, but I wouldn't go into how they are processed. The same with the cattle, but I'm positive you won't want to hear what they go through before you eat that delicious steak."

Today went fast with horseback riding and all the food processing, but today wasn't quite over yet. In a few hours there will be a barbecue. Large Steaks, baked potatoes, sour cream, chives, soup, sheepherder bread food fit for a king, with this kind of service the girls may not want to leave the ranch. However, they both left the job that's waiting for them when they return home.

After a great steak dinner, they had one more glass of wine and thanked Jack and Fred for their excellent hospitality and drove away toward home after a delightful Saturday.

The girls never brought up the Sunday picnic. They had a very long and joyful but trying day. They spend Sunday just lounging around their house and preparing for Monday's workday.

Monday morning Brenda got up at 6:30 to prepare for her 8:30 shifts. Showered and got dressed like every other day. She started down the steps to have breakfast. When she tripped on the carpet and went tumbling down the stairs. She tumbled and turned, hitting her head on the stanchions that support the handrail. Mrs. Patterson was in the kitchen preparing Brenda's breakfast, hearing the noise she ran to the stairway to find her daughter laying at the bottom of the stairs. She had blood on her face and head. Her leg was twisted, and it looked like it might be broken. Her mom began to cry, but even in her anguish she had the presence of mind to call 911. Soon there were police and ambulances in front of the house.

The ambulance attendants put Brenda on a gurney and wheeled her away, her mother by her side. When they arrived at the hospital, they told the emergency doctor to take her to the emergency room. where she was given a quick checkup.

The emergency doctor told him to get her up to the third floor where she could get an efficient Check out. Tell the doctor I said to do an MRI. Ordered the doctor.

When they wheeled her up to the third floor, every nurse on duty noticed it was Brenda. They turned into the MRI room and immediately prepped her and started scanning. It was her head they were most concerned about, but she had other less serious injuries.

After the MRI and a few films of her leg and feet. They moved her to room 309 where she would stay for a few days.

Marla is working the same shift but was unaware that Brenda was in the hospital, well at least injured. She thought she hadn't arrived at work yet.

Marla asked an attending nurse if she had seen Brenda. She said, "I've been looking for her all morning, she didn't happen to call in sick, did she?"

"Oh," Lilly questioned. "Haven't you heard? she came in earlier by ambulance."

"Ambulance, what do you mean I'll have to check at the desk and see if they know what room she's in."

Marla went over to the nurse's desk and inquired about Brenda. The nurse behind the desk told her she was in room 309, they just moved here a few minutes ago."

"Brenda, what happened to you? I looked all over the hospital for the past two hours. I guess I would have never found you If not for Lily, she said you were into 309 after your MRI. What were they testing for?"

Brenda answered, "I think in my head, not really sure I was out most of the time."

About that time a male nurse came into the room, "well young lady we're taking you downstairs."

"Now what?" Brenda asked, wondering why they brought her upstairs just to take her back down again.

"We're going to put a cast on that leg of yours. We will bring you back up so you can rest shortly after we've cast your leg."

"What about my head?" She questioned, concerned that the doctor wasn't telling her everything.

"The MRI results haven't come back from the lab yet. Don't worry, you'll be the first one to know."

Marla said, "about that leg your limp can't be any worse than it was when you climbed down off that horse the other day."

"Not funny, Marla," Brenda said, "I'd rather wander around bowlegged. I am a little sore and I have to drag my foot."

Marla held her hand for a moment, then said, "I have to go to work. I'll look in on you before I leave after my shift."

The doctor came into the room about 7 PM. He asked, "how are you feeling Brenda, did you get some sleep?"

"Not much." She returned, "what about my head? Do I have a brain?" She asked, being facetious.

The doctor laughed slightly and said, "Everything checked out good except there's one thing I'd like to check out and I need to do another MRI and look a little deeper and I don't really expect to find anything, but I have to look to make sure."

As soon as the doctor left the room. Marla walked in.

"Are you still here? your shift was over half an hour ago. I thought you were on your way home by now."

"I just hung around and worked on my records intentionally so I could come and see you before I leave. I don't have anything going on anyhow."

"I guess you're worth hanging around with and I was going to invite you for dinner." Brenda said with a hearty ho ho.

"I'd rather eat worms instead of sitting here with you, see you tomorrow."

Marla passed the Patterson's on her way out. They hugged in the hallway and briefly discussed Brenda's situation; they shook hands and goodbye.

CHAPTER 5

A MIRACLE FOR MARLA

Marla went straight home. Normally, she would've stopped and gassed up the car, maybe played a lottery ticket. While she was standing in line waiting to buy her lottery ticket. She happened to be an old male friend from her senior year in high school and her first year in college.

"Well, for heaven sakes If it isn't Brett, fancy running into you here."

"It is quite a surprise; you haven't changed one iota. Just as beautiful as ever. What's your secret?" He questioned, amazed at how pretty she was after four years. "You look like the same beautiful young lady I fell in love with all those years ago."

"Oh, come on, Brett, love? You're not serious. I bet you have women all over you." She said in disbelief.

"I'm betting you won't believe me, but I haven't dated one time since I last dated you, I promise. I've been so in love with you. I can't look at another woman."

"Brett, I'm so sorry. I didn't know you felt that way, you were the most popular male of the high school and college. I always enjoyed your company." Marla said, trying to ease the pain.

"Would you still go out with me? I mean, I'd love it if you would have dinner with me tonight." Brent said, almost begging.

"I'd love it Brett. At what time? Since it's Friday, I don't have to work tomorrow. Yes, I'd love it. Just tell me what time and I'll be ready; do you remember where I live?"

"Are you serious? I drive by several times a week just hoping to get a glimpse of you."

"Oh, Brett, don't say that you're making me sad, I really hate myself for what I've done to you, but I'm sure I told you all that on our last date at the end of graduation."

"I think I told you at the time, I would never date again until I finished college and worked a couple years as a nurse, I didn't want to waste my education. I was afraid I might fall in love and there goes all the time and money spent for college, well I've been there three years, so I guess it's okay."

"That's great," Brett said. "Will 7:30 work for you right? And thank you so much for going with me tonight, but I have something to tell you you're going to hate me for but my life's an open book I followed you home twice just to get a look at you."

"That was you? I was scared half to death. She said a little frustrated because of the act, but I recovered." She declared.

"I'm so sorry, Marla, Brett said, "I really meant no harm to you. I can never hurt you. I promise I'll make it up to you tonight."

"Forget it Brett, I have besides your intentions were pure, I will not hold it against you I promise." She ended with an apology.

"How did I ever let you get away, you're the most precious person in my life? What do you call it even, and just enjoy a great night together?"

"Wait until I see Brenda tomorrow, boy is she in for a surprise."
"I thought you didn't have to work tomorrow?" Brett questioned.

"I don't but I will certainly go by tomorrow, and I've got an idea why don't you go with me and we'll ruin my surprise?" Marla said, "Well, I better get going if I'm going to be ready by 7:30."

"Well, you know Brett, we seem to have strong feelings for each other, so you never know. I just might move in with you, what would you think about that?" she questioned being serious. "Okay, I'm gone. It takes a woman a while to get dressed?"

They hugged, said goodbye and parted company. Marla was so excited she could hardly wait to get home and tell her mom and dad; will they be surprised.

Brett walked Marla to her car and opened the door for her allowing her entrance. Oh, how Brett wanted to kiss her good night, but he couldn't afford to push it.

Marla drove away leaving Brett standing in the parking lot. She walked into the house; her mother was in the kitchen having a cup of coffee. Dad was in his favorite chair in the living room having a glass of wine. She went into the kitchen first, "Mom, you'll never guess who you ran into today?"

"It must be someone special for you to be so excited." Her mother said.

"Do you remember Brett Conklin? He was my last date in senior high school and in college in fact, he was my last date. Period."

"Oh yes dear, that very handsome young gentleman that used to bring me flowers every time he came to take you out, how could I forget him?"

"Well, be prepared, he's picking me up at 7:30, we're going out to dinner.

She went into the living room where her dad was sitting in his favorite chair, reading the newspaper. He looked up through his glasses, "well hello sweetheart you look happy. What's with the big smile?"

"Well dad, I have a date tonight."

"A date, you haven't been on a date in years, who's the lucky man, he is a man, right? Just kidding sweetheart."

"Brett Conklin," she blurted out.

"Really, he returned, is it the same Brett you dated in high school and college? He was a very nice young man, very polite, cool, calm and collected.

"I know dad he's great?" She said excitedly.

"Well, sweetheart if it makes you happy then I'm very happy for you, I haven't seen you smile like this in a very long time."

"I know so I'm excited, I can hardly wait. Sometimes time goes so slowly. I guess it's only when you're in a hurry. But when you're working, it seems like the day will never end."

"I know, dear Just relax and your date will be here before you know it, a young man will come knocking on the door, just be patient."

Marla decided to get dressed and pay Brenda a visit before she went on a date. She had plenty of time. What a better way to kill time and spend it with your friends.

She pulled into the hospital parking lot, parked and entered the building. When she walked down the hallway all eyes were on Marla, she was dressed in a beautiful attire and most of the nurses had never seen her so radiant.

Some nurses would step up and compliment her on her gorgeous dress and others would comment on her looks and ask, "your dressed as though you have a hot date!"

"You guessed it," she replied.

Brenda almost fell out of bed when Marla walked into the room. Marla just for kicks modeled like she was on the runway alongside her bed.

"Okay gorgeous, who's the lucky guy? Do I know him?"

"You sure do it's none other than Brett Conklin, do you remember him?"

"Are you kidding, you bet I do. He was the most handsome man in school. Of course, you were always the lucky one to date him. Sit down and tell me all about it."

"Well, Marla started her saga, we ran into each other at the store and it was an instant connection. We sat and had a couple of coffee and he asked me out to dinner tonight. It was just like old times again. I feel like a Renaissance woman."

"I suppose we're back to dating, wouldn't you say Marla?" Brenda asked with a facetious smile.

"I'll have more to tell you tomorrow after my date."

They conversed for more than two hours. Finally, Marla said, "I have to go. The time is getting near and I want to be there when Brett knocks on the door."

"Oh, you'll be getting out of here soon Brenda and maybe we can double date. I'll ask Brett if he has a friend as good-looking as him that would like to date a lovely lady like you, okay? But for now, I must get going, I will see you soon. How did your MRI show any problems?"

"No, fortunately they were just bad bruises more like knots."

Marla bent down and hugged Brenda, "I'll see you tomorrow Brenda!" Marla said as she headed towards the door.

"You'd better." She returned with a smirk.

Martin left the hospital, headed for home to prepare for her date with Brett.

She was nervous as an ant on a hot rock.

By 7 PM she was a wreck, it seemed to her that time would never come, but it did.

7:30 sharp, the doorbell rang. "Would you get that mom, please."

"Okay sweetheart calm down; the nervousness will soon be over." When she opened the door, Brett was standing in the doorway holding two bouquets of roses, one for mom and the other for his date, Marla.

"Well, Brett, where have you been for all these years, it's so nice to see you. Come on in. Marla is as nervous as a chicken in a coop pen full of foxes."

"Oh Mrs. Fletcher, she couldn't be that nervous, we've known each other all these years. Why all of a sudden would I make her nervous?"

He put his hand over his mouth to silence his voice saying, "I'm I'm a little nervous myself but don't let her know."

When Brett walked into the house Marla was in the living room with her father.

Mr. Fletcher, noticing Brett's coming into the room began to stand, "no-no Mr. Fletcher, keep your seat I'll come to you."

"Thank you, Brett, You always were a gentleman."

Brett walked up to Marla and handed her a bouquet of roses. After handing her mother one at the door.

"Well Marla, we have a reservation at 815 so we had better get going." She agreed and he took her by the hand saying good night to the Fletcher's. Little did they know as it would turn out that good night was for real.

"Take care of my little girl Brett. She's all we have." He said in all seriousness.

"Don't you worry about that sir, she's in good hands." He guaranteed. Mr. Fletcher was probably thinking, that's what I'm afraid of.

They drove away for a night of adventure; one they would long remember. "Where are we heading there, slick?" She liked to tease.

"We're going to a new restaurant across the town, they just opened two weeks ago. Looks like a nice place. I'm sure you're going to like it."

They pulled up in front of the restaurant where a valet opened the door for Marla and then went to the driver side and handed Brett a ticket to redeem his car after they were ready to leave the premises.

Brett escorted his lovely date through the door where they were met by a young lady who asked Marla for her wrap. She took Marla's wrap and handed her a redemption ticket.

They stopped at the desk and identified themselves and were escorted to a table.

"Will be having wine this evening, sir, or would you rather have something else? " asked the maître d', "I'll send the waiter over soon."

Brett ordered a bottle of their best wine. Soon the waiter returned with the bottle and two glasses. "That dinner waiter will be with you shortly. He said as he turned and walked away."

They had a great dinner of steak and lobster with all the trimmings. At 9 PM a band came to the stage and began to play soft music. There was a small dance floor and front of the bandstand. The two danced a few tunes before they decided to leave for the night. That is, after just one more glass of wine.

They left the restaurant, Brett asked," where would you like to go now the skies the limit. I've got it Marla, why not go to my house and have one drink. There and I will regretfully take you home."

"Well, can I trust that you want to take advantage of me?" She asked. Learning through the words.

"I promise Brett declared am I not a gentleman?"

"Okay, you win. Let's do it, I mean go to your house." She laughed at her comment that she did want to leave the wrong impression. I think Marla was a little tipsy. By the time they arrived at Brett's house. Marla was already in bad shape. No telling what will happen from there.

Brett went around and opened the car door for Marla. He helped her into the house and set her down on the couch. "Wait right here

I'll pour the wine then I'll give you a grand tour, what else could she do she was almost down for the count."

By the time Brett got back with the wine. Marla was asleep on the couch.

He tried to wake her, but to no avail, she was out like a light.

Now what do I do? He wondered; I can't take her home like this and I sure as hell don't want to call her parents, so he did the next best thing that came to mind. He went into the only bedroom, folded back the covers and then for the task of the day, and that was carrying her into the bedroom. It's tough Deadweight, but he managed.

He finally made it through the bedroom door, across the room and later gently down on the bed. He removed her dress and laid it across the back of the chair next to the bed. He then pulled off her shoes and put them under the bed and pulled the covers over her, kissed her on the four heads and left the room, closing the door behind him. He was thinking about waiting until morning, when he attempted to explain this one. On the way back to the couch. He pulled two blankets down from the hallway closet. Brett tossed them on the couch and went back to the bedroom and grabbed the extra pillow from the bed and returned to the couch to contemplate the morning and how he was going to explain to Marla that nothing happened to her, except sleep.

Brett got very little sleep, but soon it would be out in the open and everything would come to light. It seemed to him that he had just finally fallen asleep when all the sudden there was a semi-loud scream coming from the bedroom.

Brett jumped to his feet and ran to the bedroom; Marla was sitting up on the bed choking and sort of attempting to examine herself.

Red asked, "What's the matter, did you have a bad dream?"

"How did I get in your bed, and what else should I know about?"

He said, attempting to explain," I put you in there, you were asleep on the couch and I could just leave you there. So, I carried you into the bedroom and put you in bed. Did you not sleep well"?

"Yes, she replied. I slept fine, but that's not the point. How did I get undressed today?"

"Well, as you can see, I removed your dress so it wouldn't get all wrinkled and I laid it across the chair, you see it right? He said, pointing to the chair, your shoes, I put under the bed so you can see, it was all innocent. If the two of us are ever going to get together sexually it will certainly be consensual. Stopping at that, are you asking if we did it?"

"I'm asking if you took advantage of me while I was out?"

"Come on Marla you know I would do anything like that. I love you too much to screw things up by taking advantage of you. Besides, I could get arrested for sexual assault. You could put me in jail for an awful long time but that was not my reasoning. I did nothing at all out of respect for you. You'll notice you still have your slip and underwear on. Perhaps you can explain something to me that I've been wondering about for a long time."

"And just what might that be?" She questioned.

How is it under these circumstances that a woman does not know if she had sex or not, I mean there's got to be some kind of indication, like maybe soreness or some other symptoms."

"I can answer that Brett; I don't have a clue. I've never been in this situation before. Therefore, I will have to give you the benefit of the doubt."

He reached over and kissed her lightly on the lips. Thank you, sweetheart, for trusting me, you will never regret it. He concluded.

Brett reached over with his hand and patted her on the cheek, he said," get up and take a shower and I'll go fix breakfast. It'll be ready before you are, I promise."

Marla said, "are you going to clear the room first or do I have to shower in front of you?"

"Well, now that you mentioned it. It is a novel idea. However, it is not one either one of us could live with. So, let's scratch that one to get on with the day." He turned and walked out of the bedroom towards the kitchen, stopping by the couch and folding up the blankets returning him to the closet. I guess she was about to witness Brett's culinary arts.

20 minutes went by. Marla came out of the shower and got dressed a little skeptical about showering and had to put the same underwear back on again, but she really didn't have a choice.

When she walked into the kitchen. Brett handed her a cup of coffee. He said, "Let's do this right, good morning sweetheart, did you sleep well?"

She began to laugh, "You're as nutty as I remember you being back in college and I like that. It's one thing I always liked about you, your humor."

"But I was being serious, I wished every morning was like this one. I don't mean after going through a night like we did last night. What I meant was, I wish you were here forever."

Brett reached over and pulled her close to him and kissed her fervently on the lips and she reciprocated, it was almost like sealing the deal.

"Seriously Brett would you have me if I said I'd like to move in with you or am I being a little pushy." She asked quizzically.

"Pushy, he asked. I'd give anything if we can make this happen. I've been lonely for a long time and I think I've been waiting for you all at times in fact, I know I have. And now that you're here. I'd wished I'd not ever have to let you go." After breakfast, Brett took Marla home, he wasn't too anxious to see the folks, but it was the gentlemanly thing to do.

"Oh, don't worry about it, of course, the overnight sleeping arrangement may be tough to explain to dad. But then you can handle it. That's what I love about you. You have a slick tongue that can talk your way out of anything."

"I hope you're going to help me explain. Brett said, almost begging. I hope that your dad isn't here. And did I hear the word love in your last sentence?"

I've always loved you Brett, I was just never in love with you, but with a little luck, that just might change. It sure is moving in that direction." Marla said, I think she's serious. Now I'm wondering if she's happy that they cross paths in the store. This may well be what they both have been wanting for a long time.

They walked up to the front door. Her mother was standing on the other side in anticipation of their arrival.

"Marla, where have you been, I know not to worry as long as you're with Brett, especially knowing the hours that you have to work you often come home late, but then that's because of your shift and you did work last night."

"Allow us to enter and I'll do my best to explain the situation." Ted said. "I am sorry Brett, come on in, then please, I didn't mean for you to stand outside because you know here, your family." They all went into the kitchen where Mrs. Fletcher served coffee. So far Marla hadn't said a word, she was going all in allowing Brett to handle it.

"Your mom is really a beautiful person, I thought after last night, she might be livid."

"No, not my mom, she's really cool. I've rarely seen her angry." "I watched your dad; is he cool as well?" Brett asked.

"He is just like mom; they have a theory like 'stay calm and you'll never have a need to get angry.' They think things over before they act." "Good thing, does that mean if we slept over together, he wouldn't get angry?"

"Don't push your luck there. Brett!" Marla suggested.

"Why don't we go by and see Brenda. Then we can have a late lunch, no wine."

"No wine, what kind of lunch. Would that be without wine?" She laughed, "Okay, you when I waited till I got out of this dressing, take a shower. I'd love a visit with my oldest friend."

Brett sat down at the kitchen table and visited with Marla's mom while she showered and got dressed. I think that we will become best friends. I know that Brett plans to marry her. But I wonder how she feels about the situation.

Soon Marla came strutting into the kitchen looking as gorgeous as ever. "What do you think Brett and I dressed appropriately for a hospital visit? She asked, turning around holding her skirt out with both hands as if she were modeling. I think she was teasing, and it was working.

The two said goodbye, and closed the door behind them. Brett took Marla by the hand, she gave no resistance, just a smile. It had a different effect on Brett, the chills ran down his arm, looks like love really is evident.

"Your mom is really a beautiful person. I thought after last night, she might be livid after staying away all night."

"No, not my mom, she's really cool. I rarely see her angry." Marla explained.

"About your dad, is he cool as well?" Brett asked.

"Just like mom, they have a theory, stay calm and you'll never have a need to get mad. Just think things over before you act."

"Good thing, does that mean if we slept together, he wouldn't get angry?"

"Don't push your luck there, Brett." she warned. "Why don't we go by the hospital and see Brenda and we can have lunch someplace, no wine?"

"No wine, what kind of a lunch with that be without any wine?" She laughed. "Okay you will wait until after eight."

Marla started to open the passenger side door. "Wait a minute, sweetheart. Gentlemen don't stand by idle and allow a lady to open her own door. That's a gentlemen's job." Brett declared.

She stepped back in wonderment, Marla, as beautiful as she is, was not raised with chivalry. They were more modern.

"Thank you, Brett. Can I expect that kind of treatment all the time?"

"Yes, ma'am, you certainly can for me, I intend to wow you eternally. Who knows I may even ask you to marry me one day? So, I want you to think the best of me at all times."

"What makes you think that wowing me will make me want to marry you?" I don't think she was being serious.

"Because, you love me as I love you."

Nothing more was said at this point I guess they were going to dwell on it for a while.

They entered the main floor of the hospital and took the elevator up to the third floor, down the hall to room 309 where Brenda was snoring away.

Agnes, the attending nurse, was standing over Brenda talking loudly and using some terrible language. Bad, bad enough to embarrass a pirate.

"What's the matter with you nurse and when do you get off using that kind of language." Brett said, demanding an answer. Her foul mouth impropriety doesn't come close to her behavior.

"Are you alright? Brenda," Marla asked, concerned that Agnes might have harmed her.

"Oh, I'm fine. That crazy bitch just likes to let off steam, so how are you two, did you have a great date last night?"

"It was tremendous, Brett got drunk, put his hands all over me." All this time, Brett was pointing his finger at his four heads, indicating that it was Marla that got drilled, not Brett.

"Really Marla, you really got drunk. I never seen you drink enough to get drunk, wow."

"Well, Brenda, I'll take responsibility for getting drunk. I kept forcing the wind down her throat. The next thing I knew she was out like a light. I guess the next thing out of her mouth is that I took advantage of her." That got him a punch in the arm.

"Oh Marla, you know, that didn't happen." Brett said laughingly. "Yeah, when hell freezes over." She returned his laughter.

"I guess we'll have to turn down the thermostat."

"Why don't you two get a room?" Brenda chimed in.

"That's a novel idea, Brenda, but I'm afraid only one of us agrees with you. But if we talk about it long enough, I might come around." He laughed. "Did we come here to visit or talk about our," "Never going to happen?" Marla snapped back. She caught herself. She was actually beginning to get mad until realizing everyone was joking.

"Well Brett, we better go for dinner, I have to work tomorrow, so let's get out of here, soon. Brenda and I will double dare and go dancing." Marla said it like a poor joke.

"Of course, Marla I don't know if I'll ever be able to dance again, or even if I remember how, I hope this leg doesn't change my life."
"Get some rest and the dance will happen." Brett said as though it was a guarantee.

CHAPTER 6

MARLA MOVES IN

Marla and Brett left the hospital passing Agnes on the way out. As they got close, Brett pinched his nose with his fingers, making sure Agnes saw him. He got a middle digit for his gesture. All Marla could do to hold back the laughter.

"Well, sweetheart, where do you want to go now, are you hungry?"

"Yeah, I could eat a morsel. Besides, we had breakfast late, but where should we go? You have a place in mind?" Brett said.

"I'll just drive around, so something comes up."

"I know, have you ever eaten at Frank's bar and grill, Brenda used to work there. In fact, all the way through college and beyond. And the food is good."

The two walk in through the front door. The usual lunch crowd was present. They took a seat at a booth and ordered lunch. Marla ordered half a sandwich and a cup of soup, Brett had a club sandwich and a beer.

They spent most of lunch talking about Brenda and how they felt for her not being able to enjoy the same happiness that she and Brett shared.

"As I said, Brenda used to work here for three years. In fact, all the way through college, then when she turned 21, Frank put her behind the bar, which was good for tips but changed her hours, making it more difficult to keep up with the saloon and work at the hospital at the same time." Marla finally ended her tale about Brenda the bartender.

"Wow," Brett said, "that must've been hard on her, but she appears to be better now."

"Well, slick, what would you like to do now? I could take you out to the ranch and go horseback riding, Brenda and I know the Cowboys around the place."

"Yeah, I bet that would go over big. How big are these cowboys?"

"I don't know, but I'm sure they can handle themselves. All right." She said, giggling a little.

"Why don't we just go to my place. We can finish that bottle of wine and catch up on the good old times we missed out on; what do you say, partner?" He just tossed that in.

"I guess you don't like my idea about going horseback riding huh?"

"Well, it would be all right some other time, but it would be nice if I knew the hosts; I mean the cowboys, of course."

"Oh, you'll like Jack. He's a real nice guy, very quiet and accommodating. You get along with them just fine."

"We mean them. I'll urge Mr. Jack." Brett questioned.

"Well there's two of them actually, Jack and his partner. By that, I mean working partner." She began to giggle, thinking he got the wrong impression.

Well my dear will cross that bridge when we come to it. However, I think I would prefer to go to a riding stable and rent a horse, and then we can go riding into the sunset with the unknown cowboy. Besides, we haven't finished our wine list. Lunch." Brett said with a chuckle.

"You would bring that up," Marla said, "and I really wanted a cool glass of wine." I think she was teasing.

"Okay, let us have a glass of wine. I'm sure one glass will make you drunk."

"I was just pulling your leg. Brett, I don't really want a drink." She said, but I think she really did. But will she give in and go to his house we'll have to wait and see.

They finished their lunch. Got up from the table and Brett went to the counter, paid the bill, then walked back and left a hefty tip.

"Brett," Marla said, "you know I love talking to you and we do have a lot of catching up on so if you want to go to your house, let's go. I'm all for it. We might even drink that bottle of wine, what do you think?"

"Sounds like a novel idea to me, let's hit the road." I wonder what Brett really had in mind was a conversation or something a little more carnal.

Brett pulled up in front of his house. She started to open the door and once again he said, "That's my job. Just set their limbic umbrella and open the door for you and quit trying to make me something other than a gentleman."

"Well excuse me, I didn't mean to insult your integrity. I'll sit here all day if you want." She said with a smile on her face.

He walked round and assisted her out of the car, took her by the hand, and walked to the house. He opened the door for her, and they stepped inside, turned right and went into the living room set down on the large couch. A.k.a. Brett's bed.

They begin to chat about high school first year in college that they shared in the dates that they had in the fun they had when they were out just doing nothing but being together talking and engaging in make-believe.

Marla said, "I thought I was going to have a glass of wine? I'm ready, for the wind that is." She was always joking around when she was going to take it seriously.

Brett got up from the couch and when it was in the kitchen, got wine glasses and that bottle of wine that barely opened the night before. He walked into the living room, set the glasses down on the coffee table in front of Marla and poured two glasses. "Well, my dear." He said while he held their glasses high. Brett made a toast to such classes. He commenced with his comical toast, "Here's to you and here's to me. Here's what we used to be now if by chance you should disagree, to hell with you, and here's to me."

Marla laughed at the comment, "so that's how it's going to be, to hell with me? And before you start apologizing. I have heard that before, but it was kind of funny." She pulled her glass toward her lips and took a sip. "That's really fine wine Brett. Usually when I go to one of my friends' houses. They give me some cheap wine but there's nothing cheap about you. Is there?"

"I'm just trying to be accommodating."

"Sure, you are slick, you think you're going to get me drunk and into bed. Don't you?" She questioned jokingly.

"Well, sweetheart, is it working? That really wasn't my idea, but keep drinking the wine to see what happens." Brett said with a wide smile.

"You know Brett, I don't have to get drunk to go to bed with you. To be honest I think I would be scared to death. It's been so many years since I've been in a carnal mood, I think I need the wine to give me the courage which is silly. I understand that you think you'd feel a little strange yourself, which vendors long for use as for me?" She questioned quizzically.

"I don't really know sweetheart, I guess we'll just have to wait and see. But I promise you one thing: you'll make the first move and I'm not saying that being overconfident is just if I move first. I'm afraid I might make a mistake doing something you don't really want to do. That'll be the end of us, and I don't want that to ever happen. My love for you is too strong. You will never find another that loves you like I do."

"Oh, Brett, you're going to make me cry, but only because I feel the same. I'm so glad we ran into each other, and to make it all so beautiful. It was by happenstance I think you just may change my life"

They talked for what seemed to be hours. They were half through the second bottle of wine. Marla got up, took Brett by the hand and led him into the bedroom. "I'm sorry that I have a sudden desire that only you can cure."

Brett was somewhat shaky himself. After all, it has been there for years for him as well and he wasn't sure where this was going, but he had a pretty good idea. I don't mean about the sex he knew that was coming was more about where they were going afterwards. After that carnal desire was finally satisfied. Will they still be together?

They stood at the footboard of the bed, embraced it for the first time, kissed vehemently, it was soon getting out of hand and there could be only one ending.

She reached down to the bottom of Brett's T-shirt and pulled it over his head. He thought this is it, there's no turning back now.

Brett took her blouse off, reached behind her and unsnapped her bra seeing her breasts made it extremely hard for him to hold back.

She dropped her skirt and his pants. They flopped over onto the bed and the rest is history. This went on for 30 minutes huffing and puffing, breaking a sweat until the ecstasy was overwhelming.

They kissed fervently until finally exhausted. Brett rolled over on his back and said, "I thought this day would never happen and it might never have without you as my partner. I've never been one to shop around. You have been on my mind for several years. Ever since we last dated, and I know now I'll love you forever."

"I feel the same way Brett, this has been a long time coming and was certainly worth the wait." She said with tears rolling down her cheek.

"It may be a little soon but consider moving in with me. We can live like this for a long time. Perhaps forever. I don't want to let you go. If it would help to beg then I'm begging."

"I will give it a great deal of consideration. I don't think it'll be a surprise to anyone that notices. Not even my family. I think they can feel the love when they are in our presence." Marla commented. "You have such a beautiful way of putting things. Is it any wonder that I love you so? Take some time and give it a great deal of consideration? I can hardly wait to have you with me all the time and I think you'll feel the same when we're together for a while," he said, "and as a gesture, we want him to have wine anymore unless we just want to drink."

They both showered together. That was a mistake because they had to hit just one more time before drying off and getting dressed. It was every bit as exciting as the first time.

"Because of work tomorrow I think it would be best if I stayed at home tonight, but it'll give me something to think about other than patients. Can't wait to tell Brenda I bet she'll be amazed. God bless her. She'll be so happy, for us. I know because we've been friends most of our lives, we know everything there is to know about each other." Marla concluded.

"Well, the love of my life, it is still early. Why don't we go see Brenda before I take you home? I wish you were already home, perhaps we can visit Brenda for a while then go to the diner, you may want to spend tomorrow at your house. But tonight, you still have the. Brett suggested.

"That's a great idea Brett, although we saw her last night, I still miss seeing her."

"Okay sweetie, I'm ready whenever you are. I intend to accommodate your every wish now on. I'll even kiss your feet if that is what you want or that's what it takes to make you happy. I feel it is necessary to talk to your parents about moving in together. Feel free, I'll even go with you if you like?"

"No, Brett, I think I'd rather do this on my own. It's possible it will get messy; just kidding. I'm sure I'll get their blessings. The only problem is I've never lived anywhere else, been with them all my life so you can see, it will be hard for all of us. She attempted to explain without Brett feeling left out. After all, it does take two to tango."

They walked hand-in-hand down the corridor, up to the elevator to the third floor in room 309 when they entered, Brenda was setting up on the edge of the bed.

"Well, Brenda, you must be feeling better today. Setting up like that. When we left last night, you were down in the dumps. What's up?" Marla asked, expecting a wisecrack.

"Yeah, I'm feeling great. It's almost like being drunk. They have me so doped up. What's up with you two happy people, Something I should know about?" She questioned.

"Well, Brett, you want to tell her? I would prefer that I do." Marla asked, apprising Brett. He never saw that one coming.

"I think you already have, however, I'll do the honors. What was I going to reveal?" Brett said jokingly. "Oh yeah, Marla and I are in love, we may even move in together. What do you think?"

"Well, let's see, you met the day before yesterday and now you are moving in together? What took you so long, and how did you draw that conclusion?" She laughed. "I think it's great. I'm so happy for you to, I really am. You're the perfect pair you always were. Brenda concluded and then," don't celebrate until I get out of here."

"That's a promise. Brenda, no celebrating without you." Brett said, "but I'm not sure I can handle two of you." That got him a hard punch on the arm from Marla. "Now, I didn't mean any harm, ma'am, I was just making a point." Brett said comically."

"Don't talk like that. You sound just like Fred." She warned.

"Fred, who's that, your cowboy? I guess Jack must've been Marla's. Well anyhow Brenda you work on getting well and then ya'll is going to a party you'll never forget. Seriously, Brenda, as soon as you get out of here we are going to become a foursome. That is if I may bring a friend of mine tomorrow night when Marla and I can come to visit. You can just sort of check him out, you know, see if you're interested. I won't say anything to him other than we're coming to visit a friend. And that I want him to come along. If you don't like what you see then I'll never bring it up again, Okay"

"I'm pretty sure under different circumstances, I can find my own date, that being once I get on my feet again." Making it known that she's more than capable of getting a man."

"I have absolutely no doubt about that. You're beautiful lady, anyone that didn't want to date you would be nuts." He assured.

"What do you say Brenda wants to give it a shot? His name is Charlie. Most people call him Chuck. He is about six to hundred 190-pounds, give or take a little, good-looking dude and has manners and I wouldn't introduce you to him if he wasn't all I said he was." Brett continued selling his friend to Brenda.

"Give me a couple of days and ask me again, okay? I have to think about it, you know, I haven't dated for years."

"No problem, I'll introduce him to Marla. She can tell you if all I'm telling you about him is true or not, but trust me, you're going to like what she sees." "Well, Brenda, we have to get going. If I'm going to feed your friend, I'm taking fer home," he said.

"I thought you two were moving in together?" Brenda questioned them, a little confused.

"We are Brenda, but Brett and I agreed to make my parents aware of it. First, don't you think that's a good idea?"

"Ooops, I guess I thought this was already set in stone."

"Nope, but I may have something interesting to tell you when I come to work in the morning." Marla explained. She bent down to kiss Brenda on the cheek, "I'll see you in the morning babe."

Hand-in-hand, Marla and Brett walked towards the elevator. When inside, pushed the down button and headed for the parking lot.

When they reached the car, he turned Marla around, her back against the car and they kissed with great passion.

"I think we better go before we do something stupid." Marla advised.

"You're so right sweetheart, really getting excited." One last light kiss, he opened the car door and helped her in. I think Brett was feeling a little down, thinking he would miss her after taking her home. Which seems kind of ridiculous when you think about it after all, they hadn't seen each other for five years. He must've missed her an awful lot, during that time.

When they reached her residence. Brett walked to the door, they embraced. After one powerful kiss. He said, "good night and good luck," he turned and walked away, never looking back.

Marla stood on the porch and watched him drive away. She then entered the house. Mom is usually in the kitchen sipping on a cup of coffee. She asked, "Mom, where's Dad? I have something to talk to you both about."

"He's in the living room, dear dozing in his favorite chair, What's so important that you need to tell us? You're not getting married, are you? and me not yet, but of course not he would be with you asking for your hand in marriage, just like you promised."

They gathered in the living room. Well Marla was about spring the news on them. "Well, mom, dad, you almost guessed it, Brett and I will most likely be getting married someday, but for the time being, he and I discussed, and we decided I would move in with him and make sure we are on the same page. But I'm sure we are, we are definitely in love with each other. Living together is just a trial. I'm sure it will all work out, but nothing ventured, nothing gained." Marla concluded.

"Well, sweetheart you have a strange way of putting it. Now I told you before, you're old enough to make your own decisions, and you know your father and I wish you the best and personally I believe you found the best in Brett."

"Sweetheart, I think the world of Brett, he'd make a great son-in-law. I can see there's love whenever you two are together. However, remind him of a promise when the time comes, he would ask me for your hand in marriage." Mr. Fletcher said with a slight chuckle.

Marla spent some of the night packing clothes and then finally got a little sleep. She had to work tomorrow morning at 8:30. It was habit she was used to, no big deal.

Marla's major shift was right on schedule, she arrived at 8:30 AM she wasn't scheduled until 9 o'clock so she had a little time to visit with Brenda.

"Well Marla, how did it go with your family? Discussion? I bet they were surprised but happy with your choice."

"You are correct, they took it almost as if they were expecting it. I'm glad they'd like Brett as well as they do, or it might have been somewhat more difficult." She explained, "I guess I better get to the locker room and put on all my uniform, my shift has started."

Marla did her normal routine, like changing bandages, cleaning wounds, helping the doctor when necessary, and anytime the operating surgeon needed. It's funny when you're occupied out fast time goes by, before you know it, she was saying goodbye to Brenda and out the door en route to her new residence.

Marla walked into what seemed to be a strange house. She had only been there twice and now here she is in her new home; it didn't feel like it at the time, but I'm sure she'll get used to it. She begins to fill the closet with her clothes, pushing his side making room for hers. The closets were very big, but they worked it out somewhere another.

Brett came home at 7 PM and saw Marla packing away. It was a little odd because the house wasn't very big, however, it was designed for two people. "Come here and give me a kiss. It has been almost 24 hours since the last hug. Not tonight, but if it's alright with you I'd like to go to your parents' house and give them a big hug. Oh, by the way I'm going to buy a bigger dresser, maybe we can shop together, what do you think?"

"I love both suggestions. I'll be here at 6:30 PM ready to go." Marla stated. "Great. I'll be here at the same time tomorrow night, we'll go to the furniture store and buy a new dresser, put it on the back of my truck and I'm sure we can get inside, we're two strong people, we'll make it happen, okay?" Brett asked, knowing well. She was willing and able. This will be their first night together as a couple.

"What do you think about dinner? Oh by the way, do you cook, not that I'm asking you to, maybe we can take turns or just work together, what do you think?"

"Well, in answer to the first part of your question, yes I can cook enough to be happy to share the kitchen duties. It's going to be difficult since we both work the same hours. However, I will do whatever it takes."

"I love your philosophy; how could we possibly fail?" Brett said with a slight snicker.

"Well, thank you, Brett, but pat yourself on the back. It was, after all, your idea." Marla returned.

"Well, love of my life, what do you say we go to dinner. We will worry about cooking tomorrow night."

They dropped what they were doing, embraced with a kiss tossed in. Brett helped Marla to her seat in the car and they were on their way. "Do you have a preference where to eat?" Brett asked. "Frank's food is good, perhaps, will feel the presence of Brenda. She spent so many years here." Brett said.

"I think that's a great idea, yes, sounds like a winner."

Off they went to Frank's for dinner, Brad asked, "What's it going to be? I mean dinner. I just can't believe we're together. You are so beautiful you make me stick out in a crowd that is as long as you're on my arm."

"Come on Brett I'm not that beautiful, well maybe," she said, reaching across the table putting her hand on his, "you know, I don't mean that, right?" She finished with a broad smile,

"Sure, you do, how can you not, every time you look in the mirror and that's fine. Just don't try too hard to impress the younger men or the old ones, for that matter. He laughingly concluded.

Brett ordered wine for the two, "you remember the first time we started our night with wine, let's not duplicate that one, let's move on to the second night that was more pleasurable." He laughed well.

"Don't expect it to repeat tonight." She giggled.

They ordered dinner and of course another glass of wine and had an extended conversation mostly about their future.

After dinner they left Frank's on the way to the furniture store to purchase a new dresser. It didn't take long to find just what they were looking for. Instead of waiting for the dresser to be delivered. They had it loaded on the back of his truck. Satisfied, they made the right choice and headed for home.

Brett went back into the driveway, making it easier to get to the front door. "You know, I was thinking we should stop by and say hello to Brenda."

"Well, one thing it's after 8 o'clock and visiting hours are over and you wouldn't want to leave that beautiful address outside the back of the truck?" Marla said, making a statement as well as a question.

"You are absolutely correct, sweetheart, I guess I should start wearing my thinking cap," was his response.

Two days passed, "Why don't you stay at the hospital and do all the work early and I'll my friend Charlie with me so he can meet you and Brenda at the same time. Don't worry, I know the right questions to ask in her presence. I promise I won't ask anything that would make Brenda uncomfortable or think I'm putting her in a situation that she can't get out of without embarrassing herself."

Marla agreed to go along with Brett's plan. She said, "That's a great idea but come to think of it, I think it's too early for company." She suggested.

"I get your point and I agree, I'm not to share our home with anyone just yet, one day we just might have a good reason for celebration I think he might've been talking about a wedding celebration."

"Okay honey, I'll wait for you at the hospital. I should go ahead and wait in Brenda's room, I won't say anything I promise."

"Sure babe, knock yourself out, not literally, we should be there for about 6:30. How do you explain to Brenda why you're not going home after your shift?" Brett questioned.

"Oh, I sometimes stay and keep her company past my shift. She will think about it." Marla explained.

"All right, dear, I'll see you then." He said goodbye. "When I come back from work."

Brett had an idea. He would have Charlie follow him home, park his car and ride to the hospital with him, that way he can ride home with Marla and Charlie could go on his way.

Brett was self-employed, he owned his own business called Conklin Tech, so in most cases he can set his own hours. He told Charlie his plan, that is the part about him following him home, he said he wanted to supervise Marla and he would like him to meet both of the ladies at the same time.

They dropped off Brett's car as planned and proceeded onto the hospital, parked the car in the lot and walked to the hospital entrance. They got on the elevator and up to the third floor. There would be a big surprise in store for the girls. That of course would be the tall, dark gentleman with a well-groomed beard. Not long, trimmed close to the face.

They actually ran into Marla in the hallway. She looked up at Charlie and held back what she really thought, then started a normal conversation.

She offered her hand to Charlie saying, "You must be the famous Charlie Brett told me about? It appears he didn't exaggerate your very handsomeness." She said, kind of stepping over the line.

Charlie had the same impressions over, "Well, I think you should dump this old reprobate and lock horns with me." He laughed. She knew he was joking.

"Well Chuck, do you mind if I call you Chuck, I'll have to take your offer under consideration." She looked at Brett and winked.

"Perhaps I made a mistake bringing you with me, Charlie. You're trying to steal my girlfriend, never going to happen. Well, anyhow." He took Marla by the arm and started to walk down the hallway, "Okay you two. Let's change the conversation. I didn't bring you with me to try and steal the love of my life." Brett said jokingly.

"Yes, sir," Chuck said, "I have to be nice to Brett since he's my boss." He explained in a humorous way.

They arrived in front of room 309, Brenda's room. Charlie opened the door for Brett and Marla then followed close behind.

"Well, look at you," Brett said. Brenda was all made up as if she was being discharged. "What's up babe you look great. Are you getting discharged today?"

"Yes, in a couple hours. Everything seemed to be okay except for having to drag this leg around." Brenda replied.

"Oh, by the way, this is Charlie, my friend, a.k.a. my employee." Brett declared he smiled at his employee scratch that. "I don't mean it that way. I mean he'd been with me longer than my other employees." He said, giving Chuck a punch on the arm.

CHAPTER 7

A POSSIBLE BOYFRIEND

Brenda offered her hand to Charlie which he took with pleasure. He was amazed at her beauty; he had only heard about her regrets bragging that she was the second most beautiful girl he'd ever seen. Guess who was number one?

"What time are you getting discharged Brenda?" Brett asked.

She replied, "As soon as my papers are ready I will be out of here like a herd of turtles like a pirate with a wooden leg."

"Great, we can all leave together. It's getting close to seven, why don't we wait for Brenda to get out of here and since we have two cars about Brenda right with Marla and we can meet at Frank's, I'm buying dinner. How's that sound? Brett asked.

"Sounds like a great idea, you always have fantastic ideas." Marla declared.

"Who is your doctor Brenda? Maybe I can give him a push. Marla suggested.

She no longer got the words out of her mouth when the doctor came through the door, given who pushed the good doctor. "You were talking about me by any chance?" He questioned with a broad smile.

"Well, as a matter of fact I was, however, I was only going to ask about Brenda's discharge."

"Okay Marla, you know the rules, take your friends out and always wait. I'll give Brenda a brief examination if everything's all right then she's free to go." Said the fine young doctor.

They did as the doctor ordered and stepped out into the hallway and waited for the doctor to complete his examination.

Soon the doctor came out of the room and said, "Okay, she's good to go."

Marla walked over to her bedside, handed Brenda the crutches and helped her to her feet and they were off like a herd of turtles. When they reached the parking lot, Charlie helped Brenda into the passenger seat of Marla's car, he closed the door and they were on their way to Frank's bar and grill.

They arrived at Frank's, when inside with a little assistance from the guys. "Can I help you now, Brenda?" Charlie asked. He was aware that she walked around the hospital room getting used to her crutches. She didn't really need that much assistance, but I'm sure he was glad to offer.

She thanked Chuck for asking but declined his offer.

They took a booth near the window, Marla scooted in first. Nearest the window, leaving Brenda the aisle because of her leg. It didn't go well with Brett, but he kept to himself.

"Wine anyone?" Brett questioned Marla about wine. "Everyone!"

"I haven't had a glass of wine in some time. In fact, ever since I was in the hospital. No questions we don't drink wine in the hospital so perhaps I'll just have two and make up for some lost time."

"That's the spirit Brenda, get back into life, you have been gone too long."

They had a good meal and another glass of wine. They discussed business and pleasure. Brenda and Charlie seem to hit it off. They talked sitting across the table from each other, Brett and Marla also conversed with a more romantic language. When the night finally came to an end, Brett paid the bill, Charlie left a generous tip.

"Charlie, I guess you are driving home without me, so I'll see you at work in the morning." Brett said.

Marla, Brett, and Brenda drove off together, the plan was to take Brenda home and surprise her parents that didn't know she had been released from the hospital today.

They pulled up in front of Patterson's residence. They helped Brenda out of the car. He and Marla walked Brenda up to the house, one on each side.

Marla said, "We are going inside to say hello to your parents. I haven't seen or talked to them for quite a while."

Marla knocked on the door and waited for someone to answer. Brenda said,"Just open the door Marla, I live here, you know."

"Yes, I do know, however, I thought it would be more of a surprise if they came to the door and saw you standing there."

"Okay, as usual, Marla, let my parents open the door if it makes you happy."

Brenda's mother opened the door, she was surprised to see her daughter standing there with Marla and two strange men.

"Well, for heaven sakes, why didn't you let us know you're getting discharged today. Your father and I would've picked you up at the hospital. However, we probably would've met Marla and your friends." She said surprised in a good way.

Charlie helped her into the house and offered his hand to Mrs. Patterson saying, "Hello Mrs. Patterson my name is Charlie and I just met your daughter a few hours ago. What a delightful person she is."

They exchanged a soft handshake and Mr. Patterson stepped up and shook Charlie's hand." Come on in all of you. Marla, we haven't seen you for a spell, how is your family?"

"You're right, dad, they're fine. You should come to dinner one night in the near future." Marla said with a dinner invitation. I'll set it up and check back with you to make sure it fits into your schedule."

"Well that would be lovely, we'd love that," Mrs. Patterson said. "In his first meeting in your schedule. We don't really have a schedule so almost any night would be good for us."

They went into the house for a few minutes and talked to the Pattersons. Most of the conversation was about Brenda and her leg. She was asked whether she suffered with the knots she had on her head?"

"No, mom, not anymore." She bent her head down and said, "feel them I think they're all gone."

"Well, they are indeed feeling better now. So glad this part of your life is over. Now you get back to doing the things you love to do, whatever that might be."

The dinner was arranged by Marla and after work the next day she went by to see Brenda to make sure the date of the dinner was acceptable for all concerned. "On Saturday night. Oh Brenda, by the way, Brett is coming. Would you like me to ask Charlie if he would like to join us? I'm sure there will be plenty of food?"

"You're not trying to push Charlie on me are you, I can make my own choice of men. You, of course, ask him if he likes a good catch, however, I'd like to date him for a while to see just how compatible we are." Brenda replied with a broad smile.

"Compatible huh, looks like you're looking for a permanent hook up." Marla said with a slight chuckle.

"No silly, I'd like to know if he's a good dancer, but in order to find that out. I'd have to first get out of this cast for a couple months." Brenda replied.

"Well," Marla said, "I guess you will have to date for at least three months, and you will enjoy every minute of it, it's obvious from the way you two were all willing each other at dinner."

"Oh, come on Marla, we were dawdling, I mean you can't talk to a person without looking at them." She corrected.

"I'm just pulling your leg, Brenda. You're right about Charlie being a great catch and you look great together."

Just as the argument was settled. It was now time to get down to the up-and-coming dinner Saturday night.

The next morning Marla went to work, she had been denied sick shift. She was only on the job a few minutes when the scheduling nurse told her to scrub down if Dr. Rick Kohler wanted her to assist him with a heart transplant, it would be a long surgery at least eight hours less complications, then it would be much longer.

Brenda would not be able to work for at least three months and only then if she could get around good enough to comply with all the duties of a nurse. They don't want to push the nurses and Brenda definitely needed to rest.

When Marla finally got home. Brett wasn't there yet, so she called her mother to question the dinner arrangements. "Mom, are you sure you're up to cooking for that many people?"

"Oh sweetheart, I'm looking forward to preparing dinner, I managed to see Brett again and I understand Brenda is bringing a friend as well. Is he as good-looking as your Brett?"

"Come on, mom, Charlie is a handsome gentleman, but if you're asking me to make a comparison, that's not going to happen." Marla answered a little perturbed that her mom would ask that knowing how she felt about Brett.

About that time Brett walked into the house. "Compared to who?" he questioned.

"I have to go mom, Brett just came home and I haven't started dinner yet, so I will talk to you tomorrow, good bye."

Marla hung up the phone and turned and kissed Brett. "Welcome home, sweetheart." home, sweetheart."

"Sorry I'm a little late but I had a project to finish and I need to get it done, so I'll be home on time tomorrow." He said apologetically.

"No big deal dear, I was late myself. I had to assist a heart transplant and didn't get home until a little after seven. I was talking to Brenda earlier. I asked her if we should invite Charlie over Saturday night to mom for dinner?"

"And just what did she say, I bet." Brett queried jokingly.

"Yeah, smart Alec, she said, of course. Have a friend to talk to, as if there won't be anyone else to talk to." Marla concluded her sentence.

"I think I know what she's going with. I think Brenda just wants to check Charlie out for further reference, I mean watch closely. I bet they're dating within two weeks!" Brett commented.

Saturday finally came, it was time for the big event. Brett loaded up their car with some of the necessities, such as charcoal for the barbecue grill, lighter fluid potatoes and just random items. The dinner wasn't supposed to be bought and paid for by the Fletcher's, that's Marla's parents, they're supposed to be the host, not the providers. At least, that was Marla's thoughts, and they certainly didn't expect the Patterson's to foot the bill. You can bet. However, Mrs. Patterson will bring a dish or two, that's just what you do.

Charlie, (since Brett invited him at Marla's request) would pick up the Patterson's and bring them to the festivities.

Brett reminded Charlie to bouquets of roses, one for Mrs. Patterson together one for Brenda. He would do the same for the Fletcher's. Except not for Marla. That wouldn't be necessary since he wasn't trying to impress her. He'd already done that.

Brett arrived first; he was carrying a bouquet of roses. Marla, who went earlier to help her mother, opened the door. She was in a joking mood, are those for me. Brett, you shouldn't have." She said laughingly.

"They are not, was his reply they're for the pretty lady of the house."

"Are you saying I'm no longer pretty?" She asked with one eyebrow raised.

"Not at all, it's just the wrong house." He said, bending over and kissing her on the lips.

"Well, I guess I can accept that." She grabbed him by the arm pulling him into the house.

"Did you talk to Charlie? If so, what's his time of arrival?"

"I think he should be here by seven. I told him to pick up bouquets of flowers for Brenda and her mom just like I did when we reunited." He stated.

"Well don't block the doorway. Come on in and meet the family."
"Your servant in a silly mood tonight who tickled your funny bone?"

"I don't know, I'm just in a good mood today. That's better than being cranky, wouldn't you agree?"

"I'm sure it is, however, I have yet to see you cranky, but I'm sure you'll do a good job of it. When it does happen." He returned the comment.

He walked through the door and into the arms of his future mother-in-law.

He handed her the flowers, "I hope you like them Mrs. Fletcher."

"Oh Brett, you don't have to bring me flowers every time, come here, I think you should concentrate more on Marla, not that I don't appreciate the flowers, they're beautiful, but I'm already taken." She said jokingly. This is a fine family for joking around. Brett thought to himself.

Soon Charlie showed up driving the Patterson family. As well as Brenda, they both brought the bouquets.

It was impressive, but Marla felt left out because Brett didn't get her flowers, but she understood they had only been together for a few days and she's satisfied with the way everything was going, love does that sometimes.

Brett and Charlie took charge of the barbecue. Well a few of the women worked in the kitchen, wine was flowing from room to room.

Marla and Brenda brought a bottle outside to the back to keep Bretton Charlie Company, and they were welcome.

They all gathered around the extended table, Mr. Fletcher on the far end while the Mrs. sat on the other end closest to the kitchen.

Charlie stood holding his class up to make a toast," may this family bring us all closer and remain forever friends." They all cheered.

The party broke up close to 10 o'clock Charlie said good night to the Fletcher's and escorted the Patterson's to the car and assisted them inside, Brenda first because of her leg and then Mrs. Patterson's.

When they arrived, Charlie asked, "Brenda would you mind waiting in the car while I walk your parents into the house?" She of course said yes, and he proceeded to help the folks to the front porch, said good night and turned and walked back to rescue Brenda. He helped her from the car and walked her to the porch. She asked if he was coming inside?

"No," Charlie said, "I think I'll head for home, I enjoyed the evening immensely and I hope we can go out sometime whenever you're ready, I'm always available."

Brenda turned around and kissed Charlie on the lips, they were both surprised. For her it was out of desire, for him it was just what the doctor ordered.

"Wow, I'm looking forward to another one of those." He said excitedly.

So, she gave him another.

"See you soon, Charlie?" She asked and went into the house.

"You sure will, lady, as soon as you give me the go-ahead." He responded.

Brenda was smiling as Charlie walked away. He turned abruptly and started back but was halted when Brenda held up the palm of her hand, "I'll see you soon Chuck." He turned and walked back to the car, climbed in somewhat dispirited, but with the knowledge that she was willing to see him again and for tonight it was all he needed.

Meanwhile back at the Fletcher's. The party was over and Marla and her love were out the door.

"How do you think Brenda and Charlie made out?" Brett asked with a question that was mis-placed.

"I don't think they made out of Love, it is the first time they have been alone together and unless Charlie works faster than Brenda's resistance nothing happened." She responded a bit snappy.

"Yeah, I guess I misplaced a word or two with that question." He replied remorsefully.

"That's okay, Brett, before long you learn my language."

"Well, at least I can count on you to be generous when it comes to sex, can't wait to get home."

"Don't expect anything, I can't promise the outcome." She said with a blank face.

"Oh baby, don't tell me this is going to be one of those 'I've got a headache' nights?" He replied with a frown.

She laughed, "That's hysterical Brett, you Sherpa's attack, but seriously, you're not going to believe it but I'm looking forward to tonight." She said with a smile.

"That's why I love you so much, we seem to always be on the same page."

They pulled into the driveway, Marla knew not to get out of the car without Brett opening the door for, he warned her many times it was a gentleman's job. And I believe she appreciated his philosophy.

Once inside the house. They sat in front of the TV and watched the news, along with the glass of wine. Tomorrow is Sunday and neither Brett nor Marla had to work. They could stay in bed if they wanted, we'll see about that.

The next morning at 11 o'clock Marla began to stretch and yawn. The yawning woke Brett. Marla began to climb out of bed when Brett caught her arm and pulled her back down and planted a kiss on her lips with a question, "where do you think you're going my love?"

"To the shower," she said, "it's it's time to rise and shine."

"Okay," he said, "you rise, and I'll shine." That was any slapper."

Brett showered and shaved while Marla shampooed her hair for the exit the bathroom, they were ready to take on the day.

"What would you like to do today sweetheart?" Brett asked.

"Well, let's see it's a beautiful day, we could go to the park." She responded.

"Sounds like a good idea, but I take you to breakfast and we'll stroll through the park when we finish eating"

That's what they did. They sought out a place a lot different from the usual. It happened there was a small café just two blocks away from the park. It was new to them, and the food was good.

After they finished eating, they left their car parked at the café and walked to the park, just for the exercise.

They found an empty table and sat across from each other to begin to talk about Brenda and Charlie, whether or not they were compatible.

"Oh," Marla said, "they look great together if that helps, but I'm sure it's apparent to both."

Afternoon extended discussion about Brenda and Charlie. They decided to walk around the park and see what was on the other side and what other people were doing. At the far end of the park sitting alone at a table were the two subjects of discussion. Brenda and Charlie.

"What the heck are you two doing here?" Marla had asked.

The response came short and quickly, "the same with you two. I guess great minds think alike. Why did you give us a call so we could have breakfast together?"

"We didn't want to bother you lovers, so we just went to the little café a couple of blocks from here and eight and then walked around the park." Charlie answered.

"Talk about great minds thinking alike. We needed to go to the same café, left the car. Learn to walk here, how's that for coincidence?"

"We were thinking about going to the lake and taking a dip, but you say, you in?" Charlie asked.

"Are you sure you want us along? Would you want to be an interloper and spoil your day, just because we're friends? I mean, we thought you wanted to be alone, but then you could get a room. In that case." Brett said, laughing like an idiot.

Brenda said, "we have got that close yet, if ever," she said, raising an eyebrow and staring at Brett in the face of his statement.

"Okay Brenda, I apologize. I was only joking." He said being sorry for his remark.

"I know you were Brett." she said, feeling sorry for her attempt to embarrass him.

Charlie spoke, "leave your car parked where it is and you two can ride with Brenda and I."

"I have a better idea," said Marla, "drop us off from Faye and will take my car home and park it in a pickup or swimsuits. They will go by Brenda's pick up yours and we're off like a herd of turtles." "Whoops, I'm sorry Brenda, I forgot, you can't go underwater with a cast on you're liable to drown."

They did as Marla suggested, and soon they were on their way to the lake. It was just a small lake up and the mountains, which is just north of the city. Not long, but a boring drive.

After arriving at the lake, they parked the car. They headed up the hill a couple hundred feet to the lake. Brett and Marla put their suits on under their clothes, so waste trip down under a tree in hunger close on aluminum and proceeded to the water's edge.

Brett brought along a rubber raft which he inflated with the tire pump.

They would take turns paddling across the lake and back.

Marla wasn't a gold-medal swimmer. So, Brett swam alongside the raft holding onto the side for survival comfort for his lover.

They spent the day and left just before dark, arriving back in the city at nightfall. After arriving at Brett's house, they said goodbye to Brenda and Charlie and went back into the house to shower off the lake. Poor Brenda, she was just along for the ride. Since she couldn't put on a bathing suit and go underwater with a cast on, she couldn't go to the water, but she enjoyed watching the rest of them having fun. I think Charlie felt somewhat guilty for suggesting going swimming without regard to Brenda's condition.

Monday morning, Marla went to work at 8:30 AM. She walked into the hospital right on schedule, Brett, on the other hand left for work at 7:30 AM but then he was self-employed and usually got off work at 6:30 unless he had a lot of work to catch up on any would be the office till 7:30 PM. Even later fee had a lot of work to catch up on.

Brenda, while scheduled for the same time as Marla was on medical leave with a broken leg at 1015. A call came from the police department. The call was directed to Detective Lieut. Kelly who in turn passed it on to Sgt. Ed Baker.

Detective Kelly said, "Ed, I just got a call stating that the local credit union was robbed. I need you to get on it immediately."

"You got it boss." Sgt. responded. He called on assistance from Sgt. Charlie Taylor.

There were only three windows open in the bank because the credit union had just opened.

Two men dressed in hoodies with masks underneath pulled up to the curb and parked the getaway car after dropping one off just around the corner of the bank. The shore one stood behind the bank on the corner waiting for the taller man to get out of the car and walk to the entrance of the bank. This drew the attention of the guard who had drawn his gun after seeing the mass bandit and started to approach them. When the short one came around the back and slipped up behind him and shot him in the back of the head. They dragged him quickly behind a hedge hiding the body.

Once inside the bank the bigger of the two walked into the office where a male employee was sitting at his desk talking on the phone.

The robber stepped inside the room gun pointed at the man's head and marched him out. He handed the man three bags, ordered him to give one to each seller and ordered them to fill them and be aware not to set off the alarm or they, along with the customers would be shot. The tellers began shuffling money into the bags.

A customer came in during the holdup and was quickly ordered to get down on the floor with the rest of the customers. Now that the robbery was in progress the guard pulled under the hedge in front of the building. It looked like smooth sailing.

Everything happened in a one-minute flat, the bags were not totally full, because there was a short timeframe.

They grabbed the bags and darted out of the bank, climbed into the car motor running and sped off.

The police arrived just three minutes later, giving the robbers that much leeway making it difficult to find them. With that much head start. They began questioning the people, "Did anyone see their faces, can you describe to them what they were wearing?" The questions were directed to everyone in the bank.

One teller added to the description, saying, "The tall one had blue eyes. I saw them through the opening in the mask." She concluded.

"Well Charlie, it appears to me it's the same as we've been trying to find for the last six months."

"Yeah, I add, I think you're right, same description in detail. Now if we knew what they were driving it could be of significant help, although the last two cars were stolen, this one was probably the same.

The last customer to any of the banks spoke, "I don't know if it means anything or not, but there was a car I noticed when I came in. I thought it was rather strange that anyone would leave your car running while in the bank."

"You didn't happen to notice the make or color of the car, any little thing could be of significant value, even if you would think it was unimportant."

"Well," she said, "it was pretty blue, looked fairly new and low on the truck was a small round plate with three colors inside the ring."

"Would you by any chance know the three colors?" The detective queried.

"Well," she said," I'm not sure but I believe in the three colors. One was blue or black. Not sure. Another one was white. I don't really know what the other one was." She concluded.

"What you think it sounds like a BMW to me."

"You're right, it looks like they're getting high class, at least the cars are newer than the ones before. Sgt. Baker."

Sgt. Baker, where's the guard? I'm sure you have one wisely not present during a robbery?"

They all chimed in at the same time, "He should be just outside the front door. That's where he usually stands right next to the ATM machine."

The officer went outside to look for the guard. It didn't take long after pulling back the hedge branches, "There he is Ed. Looks like he was shot in the back of the head."

Ed called into the office to the lieutenant in charge, they put out an APB on the car. By the time the detective got off the phone the coroner pulled up to where they were standing.

"Good morning Ed, what we have here, looks simple enough. The examination that is but will have to take the body to the lab. It appears the bullet is still lodged in the head as soon as I retrieve it. I'll get it to the lab to see what the bore is and maybe we can find a match for your bandit."

"Not a bandit, murderer." The Sgt. corrected.

"Well, Ed, it's not much we can do until the lab gives us the go." The coroner explained.

"I know Frank, but I'm desperate to find these two before they strike again."

"We'll do the best and the fastest job we can."

With that being said, had gathered up everything he had at his disposal and went back to the office. Disgusted with the entire situation, the lack of unclean evidence against these ruthless criminals is despicable, just one break, one mistake and anything to start an investigation with.

"You sound a bit frustrated there Ed." The assistant officer said.

"Damn right I am, and return frustrated you're getting impatient. My friend will get a break, almost always when we get it will burst this case wide open."

"Sounds encouraging, but I'm just so pissed at how close we get, but we never seem to get our hands on them. I feel like if we ever come in close contact, I may not be able to restrain myself from wringing their necks." Ed was a little down on himself.

Ed's companion and assistant investigator finally trim down enough to wait until the results came back from the lab. God help us. When that happens. If these results come back positive, telling where it will go with it, I just hope he calms down. This is way out of character for Ed, usually much more mellow.

The week went by and the reports came back from the lab, much to Ed's chagrin. There wasn't a match to the prior gun bore, so it's another setback. I guess we'll have to wait for another crime to be committed and hope for the best.

CHAPTER 8

MOVING FORWARD

Back in the world of Marla and Brett everything was going well, however Brenda and Charlie still hadn't locked hearts yet, but it'll happen eventually.

Brett was getting anxious to move forward with Marla and although she was in love, she still wasn't in a hurry to jump into a marriage. Brett said, "The school this weekend and look for a bigger house, what do you think?"

"I think there's only two of us and we have a big enough house for two, I mean we have a bedroom, bathroom, kitchen, all the space that people in love need." She replied.

Well what should we have an overnight guest, like Brenda and Charlie? I mean one of these days soon, we're going to connect and will have a good time with them. Besides, we can have a backyard barbecue but now we don't have much of a backyard out of this house." He said, trying to be convincing.

"Okay sweetheart, that's what makes you happy just might turn out to be fun, of course, everything so far with you is fun." Marla said with a facetious grin.

They drove around most the day in and out of houses but had yet to come across what they particularly liked. Brett said, "Let's go for the better. This section town sees how the elite live, of course, it may be above our pay grade, but it's worth a try." He looked over at her and winked.

"I'm sure with both salaries, we could afford a pretty decent piece of property." She added.

They continued to cruise around until they came to a gated community. "I think we might need an agent to look at these places." Brett said, "Take the names down some of the agents on the for-sale signs will give him a call next chance we will get in there to look at some of the better houses."

She did as Brett asked, and continued selecting houses they wanted to see from the inside, looking at the kitchens and bathrooms, bedrooms and so on.

"Yeah, I think I have seven altogether. You think that is enough?"

"Yes, enough for now, the school luncheon. Think about it over something to eat, what do you say?"

"Sounds like a wiener to me, where do you want to go for lunch?" She asked.

"You pick a place, and that's why we are here, every choice, today you're the boss." He replied.

"Wow, to what do I owe this privilege?" She asked with a snicker. "Because I love you so much. I will be your servant, at least for the rest of today" he said with a sentimental look on his face.

"That's all, just for today. What about the rest of the time, we'll be in charge then?" She questioned, still laughing.

"For a lifetime if you will marry me. (That came as a shock. She wasn't expecting it, at least not so soon.)

"Well, sweetheart, that's a great thought, but for the time being that's all it is, a thought but do not be content. I promise the way things are going now it will happen eventually." She returned with the promise.

Marla suggested a small café downtown where there would be lots of people, we haven't been in a crowd for some time. We need to mix it up once in a while." This time she ended with a wink.

"Let's do it, I'm game if you are, and apparently you are, so let's go." He said, turning the car around in the direction of the city.

They found a small but very popular café in the middle of Pleasantville, she wanted a crowd and got more than she bargained for. People were standing in line waiting outside to get in. When they finally entered the café, they waited even longer, until a voice rang out, "Conklin party two?"

They were seated at a booth near the window. It's always a nice setting at the window so you can watch the different people and how they act and converse with the other people around them.

"Well, sweetheart, what's on your menu?" He asked what she would like for a light lunch?

Her response was short and quick, "The same thing that's on yours" she said, raising an eyebrow, waiting for his response.

"Touché my dear, touché," They both laughed quietly so as not to attract attention.

Brett reached across the table and put his hands on hers, I can only imagine, life will never change for us. As long as we're weird together, and I hope that's till death do us part!"

"Oh, that's so sweet Brett, I think you will probably be proved correct, I'm in your corner." She said with a puppy dog look on her face so sweet.

"Hope you're right sweetheart, maybe after we moved into our new house we can move forward with our plans."

"We'll see, but first we have a chore in front of us, and that will be finding the right house, one of your choices, of course."

"You needn't acquiesce just because of something I want; we are in this together, come hell or high water." Brett said, vowing that everything they had would be on an equal basis.

They were enjoying the meal as well as a conversation, Brett was eyeballing the patrons when out of the blue he saw a familiar face, he just couldn't put his finger on the identification of this person. He looked across the table and said, "Marla, without staring, see the young man across the room setting with a mixed group of guys and women?"

"Yeah, so what is he? someone you used to know? He appears to be the only one without a girlfriend." She replied.

"Yeah that's the one, I know him from somewhere. But I just can't remember who or from where I know him."

They continued with their meals, still wondering who this mysterious young man might be. 20 minutes passed and the group from across the room began to shuffle around getting out of the booth and squirming through the tables lined almost to the door. It just so happened they would pass where Marla and Brett were sitting talking after their meal, except for a cup of coffee.

Just as the young man passed Brett a name came to mind. He spoke out the name "Justin". The man turned immediately and responded," are you speaking to me?"

"If your name is Justin, yes I am." Brett answered.

"Well, for crying out loud is that you Brett?" He questioned," Brett Conklin?"

"That would be me, things are beginning to come back in his mind." Now Brett said, "Is your name Justin Clark, did we share a class or two in college?" Brett asked, amazed that after all these years he would run into someone he went to college with.

"We sure did Brett, what are you up to, keeping busy? Who's the beautiful lady sitting with you, your wife?" He couldn't seem to run out of questions.

"Soon, I hope, but for now we're just exploring the opportunities. How about you, are you married or still wild as a march hare like you were in college?"

"No, I was married for a short time, but it didn't work out. I guess I was too much of a playboy to hold a marriage together, well I better go and catch up with the party I came with, hope to see you again.

"Wait a minute," Brett said he reached into his wallet and pulled out his business card and handed it to Justin.

Justin looked at the card and made a comment, "Conklin tech, huh, it appears that you got some benefits out of college, good job Brett."

"Where are you working Justin?" He asked.

"Well, I'm sort of unemployed right now, I got a couple offers to look into." He finished his sentence with, "but I have to go now, but I'll call you in a day or so and we'll catch up with old memories."

"I'll be waiting for your call Justin." With that said, he left the room to join those he came with.

"He seems like a nice guy Brett, sure it took you long enough to remember his name, but then it has been quite a while."

"Yeah, we didn't know each other very well. He was sort of a Casanova, never could keep a girlfriend, he drifted from one to another. I'll catch up with all the dirt when I talked to him, he may have changed but I doubt it, never could before. So why now?" He concluded his tale of Justin.

"Well, sweetheart, what would you like to do next?" Brett asked

"I think I'd like to take a nap, what about you, lover?" she said with a facetious grin.

"I'm not necessarily sleepy, however, I'll be happy to bed down with you anytime." He returned the facetious grin. I wonder what they actually had in mind, Naw, not an afternoon delight.

They decided instead of going home they would stop by and say hello to Brenda. While pulling up to the curb in front of her house they noticed Charlie's car alongside the curb. "Well," said Brett, "I told you they would be getting together before long."

"Okay Brett don't count your chickens before they hatch. Just because his cars are parked in front of her door doesn't mean they are there together. He probably just dropped by to say hello to her parents" she laughed knowing Brett was right on. It was Brenda he came to see without a doubt.

They approached the front door, knocked three times, stepped back and waited for an answer.

The door opened, Charlie answered, "Well to what do we owe this visit?"

"Well, actually we came by to say hello to Brenda, didn't know she had company, Mind if we join you? She knew he couldn't say no."

"Come on in I'm sure Brenda is anxious to see you two, of course I'm speaking for her." He laughed, "and you're not interfering, we're just talking over a brew."

Brett looks at Marla, shrugging his shoulders, "What you say we have a beer?" Wrong question.

"I don't say anything, I would rather drink it than talk to it." She said and Brett was just about to answer.

"Well, Brenda," Marla said, "fancy meeting you here." Another mistake.

"Really? I live here, I'd say to you 'fancy meeting you here.'" They laughed and hugged, "How's the world treating you? I miss you at work."

"Yeah, me too, I will be glad when this cast comes off, I'm anxious to get back to work."

They sipped beer and told stories from now and the past more, Marla couldn't help but notice that Charlie and Brenda were very close, thinking Brett was right, they are close and that's great now we can date as a foursome on occasions.

After an hour or so, Marla suggested that she and Brett head for home. "Getting kind of late and I have to get ready for work tomorrow."

Brenda said, "Stick around and we'll go to the diner for dinner tonight."

"Sorry girl, but we just had lunch, maybe another time in fact, let's work it out, it'll be fun."

That being said, Marla and her counterpart walked out the door, climbed into the car and pointed it in the direction of home.

It was a great day. After all, they got to house hunt, have lunch, meet an old friend and visit with Brenda and Charlie.

Now home enjoying a glass of wine and talking about the day, with a little future tossed in. It's time to go to bed and prepare for tomorrow, just another workday for both.

7 AM sharp. Marla hit the shower. "Need any help in there?" Brett asked, he knew better, Nothing ventured, nothing gained.

Brett hit the shower first. All Brett needed before leaving for work was a kiss from his future wife, and out the door he went. He was very good about being punctual. Of course, he set his own hours, but he was always at work by 7:45.

Marla had different hours, she would go to work and be on the job by 8:45, allowing time to put on a uniform and check in with the nurse's station to see what her schedule was for the day. Mondays were usually a very busy day. Too many people partying over the weekend causing accidents, or people just getting too many viruses from weekend gatherings and so on, so Marla, without a doubt, would keep busy.

Brenda is so anxious to return to work she's getting tired of sitting around the house and they won't remove the cast for another week, she has even requested desk work, but for now she's going to have to wait.

About 10:15 AM Monday Brett got a call from his one-time friend, Justin. He invited him to Conklin Tech to show him around possibly reunite their friendship.

Brett called the guard at the front gate and told him to allow Justin Clark through and direct him to his office.

Justin pulled into the gate at 11:10 AM, showed his driver's license and was told where to park and how to get to the bosses' office.

When Justin walked into the office. Brett looked up and saw him coming. He got to his feet to shake hands and told him to take a seat so that he would be with him as soon as he finished the phone call.

Brett told the person he was talking to that he would call him back shortly then hung up the phone.

"Well, Justin, how's things going?"

Justin said, "Just fine like I told you the other day I'm between jobs, but I have an interview next week."

To Brett between jobs meant unreliable, maybe incompetent, but he didn't want to prejudge so he carried on with their conversation. Brett found out that Justin was a computer technician, that impressed Brett, but he wondered why if he was smart enough to repair electronics jobs should come easy, there is plenty out there.

"Come on Justin, I'll give you a tour of my business."

He showed him all the departments, and Justin was very impressed. "Maybe I can go to work with you one of these days, I see you do a lot of electronics, of course, you do, that's what it says on the sign you're an electronic tech company."

"Will have to check you out little bit Justin, come in Monday next week and we'll go through the departments and see what you're best qualified to do. We do a lot of electronics and if that's what you're good at you should be able to pick it up in a hurry." Brett concluded.

They actually build computers and Justin is a computer expert. However, for this job he has to assemble them after making the parts.

They finished the tour and went back to Brett's office. You'll see more when you come back next week. I'll let you demonstrate your skills." Brett said maybe we can fit you in somewhere if you're really interested."

"Well Brett, I'll be here. I think I can show you a few things, I don't mean the way that that came out like I was smarter than you, if I was, I would be sitting behind the desk and you'd be standing looking down on me." They both snickered.

Justin left the office agreeing to return on Monday for an interview.

Brett returns to work. He still had several calls to make. There was lots of business to attend to before his day was over.

At 2 PM, he asked Charlie if he wanted to go to lunch with him. I'm getting a little hungry, but he wasn't sure if Charlie had eaten or not. It so happened he had not. They dined in a small café just two blocks down the street from the business.

During lunch Justin was the subject of conversation mostly about his credentials. "What do you think of Justin?" Brett asked Charlie.

"Well I'm not much of a judge of character, but he is your friend. However, with that being said, I think he's worth a shot. I mean what do you have to lose?"

"You're right, Charlie, If we don't like his qualifications, he's out of here, but he could be a welcome addition to the business."

After lunch, Brett and Charlie returned to the shop and Brett went back to work making phone calls.

Charlie was the foreman who took care of everything in the back of the building overseeing the employees. They had contract work with a few airlines but mostly they built computers. The parts they built for the airlines were very tedious and accuracy was essential, one flaw could cost the aircraft to go down and crash, not only killing people would put Brett out of business. Brett actually worked hard. It took a lot of energy twisting the arms of some of his clients. It wasn't just a phone call to clients, it took grit to accomplish all the tasks bundled up in his office. It made the day even longer, knowing what was waiting for him at home. However, he has a surprise in store for him. Marla is in the middle of an operation and couldn't leave the hospital until the surgery is complete. Just another day in the life of a Nurse.

Brett drove into his driveway, noticing Marla's car wasn't present. He wondered if she was still working.

He entered the house, popped open a bottle of wine, poured himself a glass, took a seat in the living room and waited for Marla to arrive. At 8:30 PM she walked to the door, and Brett asked, "What happened sweetheart? that's a stupid question to ask a nurse, I apologize, my dear." He, after a deeply romantic kiss, put his arms around her and danced her over to the couch and set her down, said to her "Are you up for your glass of wine after which you could explain why you're so late?"

"I can tell you right now, even without the wine." She declared, "but your wish is my command."

Brett laughed all the way to the kitchen. He returned cradling two glasses of wine, handed one to Marla and took a seat next to her on the couch. "Okay, let's hear it, no, never mind I don't doubt you for a minute. You probably had an emergency, right?"

"Well, you solved the mystery all by yourself, and yes I had an emergency just after five, but we have it all wrapped up, can we have a sip of wine now?" She asked, raising an eyebrow.

"Let's sit here and sip the wine and you can tell me all about your day, how's that?"

"It's fine, but one of us is going to have to fix dinner."

"Oh my gosh, I never thought about you being hungry, I'll fix us something right now."

"Are you sure, you must be hungry as well. Unless you have already eaten?"

"No, as a matter of fact I was waiting for you to get home, I don't like eating alone."

I've got an idea. Let's order a pizza delivered, that way neither of us will have to cook." Marla suggested.

"So, is it any wonder why I love you so much?" Brett said with a happy face. "I love the way you sugar coat everything, not necessary."

"Brett, I will always love you, so you don't have to be so sweet to me every time we're together, but I love it."

"Okay, let's talk about real estate agents, give me your list and I'll call as many as I can squeeze in tomorrow, how's that sound?" Brett questioned.

"That's a great idea because as you know what my schedule is sometimes, I get busy and I can't even make it to the bathroom." She laughed.

30 minutes and one more glass of wine, there was a knock on the door, it was a pizza delivery boy. Brett opened the door, paid for the pizza with the tip and closed the door behind him. "Dinner's here." He shouted to Marla who was still sitting in the living room sipping on her wine.

"Are we going house hunting this weekend?" Marla asked. "I think that was the plan, unless you have something better in mind, besides, that's what we got all the agents names for I believe." She stated.

"I'm kind of anxious to get inside those electric gates and circumnavigate around those beautiful homes, in fact, you might say I'm exuberant."

"Oh, come on Brett, the house is not a treasure chest. She laughed. Your friend Justin is supposed to drop by your office Friday, right? I hope he works out for you because he's your friend and maybe he will turn out to be a good worker and an asset."

"We'll see, and I'll report back to you when I get through with the meeting. However, after our last meeting, it doesn't appear that Justin has changed his way of life; we will deal with it, if he's around for a while we'll have to wait and see."

Meanwhile, Charlie visits Brenda on a nightly basis it appears on the surface they will soon join the ranks of Marlon Brett and possibly move in together and that would really make things interesting.

The week went by fast. It was already Friday and time for Brett to interview Justin. He arrived at Conklin tech at 930 sharp, ready to see if he would fit into Brett's business. He was allowed to pass through the gates as per Brett and enter the office.

Brett extended his hand, and clasped with Justin's, and they shook hands. Brett said, "The schooler back in the building I showed you some of the equipment, especially the tools we use to make the electronic parts to fulfill the contracts that we design for many things, mostly computerlike components, some for aircraft as well."

"Wow Brett, this stuff is really elaborate. I guess you have to handle it with kid gloves." He was amazed at the tools.

"Well, Brett said, is not all that delicate. I mean, you know, you have to use a certain amount of cautiousness, but it's pretty simple once you get to know what. Oh, and by the way I need you to ask you about your father. Is he doing okay?" Brett question.

"Aw, not really, although it's been a few years since mom passed, he can't seem to let go. He works a few days here and there that he stopped for a while, probably only works three days a week sometimes. I help out as much as I can buy pain mostly utilities, however, I have worked much lately."

During the conversation Charlie walked up, put his hand out. "Justin," insisted famous Justin.

"And you look familiar to know each other from someplace?" Charlie queried.

Brett interrupts, "Yeah, Charlie went to college at the same time you and I did, in fact I had them in a few of my classes."

"Well, I'll be damn, I thought you looked familiar.

By the way, Justin, Charlie will be working with you until you get acclimated, it won't take long with your electronic experience. When you and Charlie get finished, come to the office. We still have to discuss wages."

Brett went into his office and began going through the files he was looking for the contract form. He was diligent when it came to hiring people, no matter how well he knew the future employees.

Justin took a seat in Brett's office. They talked for about 45 minutes and they agreed with what Justin's wages would be and a promise. If he did what was expected of him there would be an increase in salary. "I look at the progress of my employees every three months."

They shook hands sealing the deal, Brett said, "Okay Justin be here Monday morning at 8 o'clock sharp." Justin nodded his head and walked out the door.

Brett, on his way out the building ran into Charlie. "Well Charlie, got plans for the weekend?"

"Yeah, I'm taking Brenda to the movies, you and Marla are welcome to join us. I'm supposed to pick her up at seven." Charlie invited.

Justin said, "I'm sure Marla would be delighted to spend time with Brenda, it's a great catch, and you need to spend as much time with her alone as you can. It gets a little more difficult when she has to go back to work now that the cast is off. I'm sure that'll happen very soon."

"Yeah, I think she's going back to work Monday morning. I know she's anxious, she said she hasn't missed this much time since she became a nurse. That's almost 4 years ago.

"Wow, I hope Justin can have that good of a record, four years without time off even for medical leave. That's amazing, but I guess you can call it commitment to your job. I know she and Marla are dedicated to their jobs."

"I can't help but hope Justin is as well." Brett said finishing his statement. "Well Charlie, I got to go, Marly's probably home by now, I wonder what she's planning for dinner?"

"I guess living together has its benefits, maybe Brenda and I will be in that kind of a relationship someday." Charlie said, "See you Brett. Gotta go home and take a shower before I pick up Brenda."

"How are you getting along with the Patterson's?" Brett asked. "Great, I'd say, I mean they call me son, how's that for starters?"

Brett pulled up to the curb in front of his house, Marla's car was in the driveway. I guess he knew who the boss was in this relationship. It was Brett's idea in the first place. So, Marla wouldn't have to move his car to go to work since Brett leaves earlier. He goes to work at 7:30 so he pulls in behind her, but since she doesn't have to leave as early as him. That's the reason those arrangements were made.

When Brett went in the house Marla was waiting behind the door; he closed the door and there she was. She grabbed Brett around the neck putting their lips together in a lovelock, "Welcome home." She said, "If I had known I would get this kind of surprise I'd sneak in more often." Brett said jokingly.

"Oh, come on Brett, you don't have to sneak in, I'll be waiting for you wherever you are. You like surprises, Don't you?" She questioned.

"I like your kind of surprises. I'll take them any time." They held hands and walked into the kitchen. Brett took a seat at the Island counter while Marla poured two glasses of wine and then asked him, "do you like beef stroganoff?"

"I love it, is that what I smell. If the stroganoff tastes as good as the aroma, we're having a great dinner and it's my personal favorite."

"I'm glad you like it so much. However, it's the only meal I know how to make." She said jokingly.

"Oh, come on babe, I've tasted other dishes you've made before, and they were all delicious." He complimented her.

After they finished dinner, Brett helped with the dishes. She poured two glasses of wine and retired to the living room. They sat next to each other, turning on the TV and scanning the channels.

"How many agents did you contact, and when do we get to see our first house?" Brett asked.

"Well, I'll have to look at my notes, I believe 11 o'clock at 327 Partridge Ave., funny name for Street." She commented.

"Well said Brett, it should be easy to remember, I used to hunt Partridge, a good eating bird."

"Yuck, did you really eat Partridge, where do you find enough pear trees for hunting? Partridge?" She asked, questioning his statement.

"That's just a myth, sweetheart, they don't live in Trees. They live in the brush, as do many birds." He reiterated.

"Oh well, what you say we go to bed. It's about that time?" I'm sure he wouldn't have a problem with that.

"Sounds good to me, we can get up, shower and get an early start by having breakfast at the café close to our destination."

"You're so smart, that's why I love you so much." Marla said. (sure, sounds like I hear wedding bells.)

CHAPTER 9

A HUNTING WE WILL GO

They did as Brett suggested, went to bed and continued their conversation.

Up early the next morning, showered, played around a little, then got dressed and headed for the café.

"You're not going to believe it Marla, but isn't that Charlie's car parked over there next to the black convertible? What are the odds." Brett asked.

"I don't know," she replied, "but it's great that we can have breakfast with them, they must think like us."

"Well, there's a car pulling out just three cars from Charlie's. I'll park there, you want me to let you out in front of the café?"

"Yeah, when I'm in my 80s." She laughed, "I'm pretty sure I can keep up with you!"

"I was just being polite." He answered, "You're always polite, how long must I wait to see your dark side, everyone has one you know,"

Marla asks. She never really cared. It was just a question to extend the conversation.

"What about you, do you have a dark side? He asked. Returning her question.

"Well, I have a great restraint so I promise if I have, you will never see it, fair enough?"

They took a seat in the booth with Brenda and Charlie and had a great breakfast. They gobbled the food down much faster than planned but then they had an appointment with the real estate agent.

After a short conversation and finishing her breakfast, they took off in search of a new house.

"I really enjoy having breakfast with Brenda and Charlie, don't you Marla?"

"Yes, they're great, but you just passed the house we were looking for." She said, giggling.

"Oops," he said, making a U-turn in the middle of Partridge Avenue. He pulls up in front of the gate, it opens, and they enter as per the agent inside awaiting their arrival.

The agent motioned them to come to the end of the street where the house in question engulfed the entire cul-de-sac.

They shook hands with the lady agent, and she led them into the house. "Oh, Brett, this is beautiful, four bedrooms, three bathrooms, living room, kitchen, and even a den, beautiful, what about the price?" She questioned.

The agent said, "This beautiful piece of property is only $300,000."

Brett said, "it sounds like a lot, but it has great features. However, with that being said, I don't think we want to jump into the first house, we have a few more to check out, but I guarantee you we will give you an answer soon."

They shook hands, Brett, Marla, climbed into the car and left the premises and went to another location. They spent the rest of the day looking at houses, some were more impressive than others, but number one seemed to be the favorite.

They took a lunch break and discussed the possibilities, but always coming back to the first house is definitely their choice.

Marla asked, "Do you think $300,000 is too much Brett? I don't know if that's beyond our budget, what do you think?"

"No, sweetheart. I'm sure we can afford it however; let's go back and talk to the lady, maybe I can talk her down."

"You're the boss, if you think we can handle it let's do it, it's so spacious it'll take some time to get used to but will manage."

"You're not happy where we are?" Brett asked jokingly.

"Of course, I am, if we spent the rest of our lives in a one-bedroom house It's fine with me, we have everything we need, especially together." She said,

They stopped at the phone booth just outside the café, called the real estate agent, and made an appointment for that very evening at 7 o'clock.

They pulled up to the gate which was quickly opened, they passed through and was escorted into the house the agent said, "It's a hard place to leave once you've seen it, isn't it, Mr. Conklin, do you want to look around some more?"

"No," Brett said, "I think it's time we talk. What's your best offer? Marla and I are having a tug-of-war between this place and one other, they're both beautiful, so let's get down to business."

"Well, Mr. Conklin, prices are very reasonable, I'm not sure how much less the owner is willing to go but ask, how can I get in touch with you later?"

Brett reached into his pocket and pulled out his checkbook and wrote a check for a hundred and fifty thousand dollars and handed it to the agent, "tell your client you have this when the price comes down to $290,000 then give me a call." He gave her a number where they can be reached after 8 AM tomorrow.

They shook hands and Brett and Marla walked away, got into the car and drove off.

"Do you think she'll call Brett?" Marla asked.

"I'd bet my life on it." He said in answer to her question. "Pretty sure of yourself, aren't you, dude?"

"Well, you have to understand I deal with people on a daily basis. I have to press hard sometimes to take control, so I know what the breaking point is."

"Sounds good, shall I ask Brenda if she wants to go with us?"

"Only if she's with Charlie. That way we can have a lot of company and they are always fun together."

"I guess you're right. After all, you haven't seen Charlie since yesterday."

Okay, forget it was just a suggestion." she said, almost disgusted. They called anyway but she and Charlie were out to dinner according to the Patterson's.

"That sounds like a plan to say we go to Charlie's and have dinner?" Just as it happened once before when they pulled into the parking lot at Frank's bar and grill there was Charlie's car so it appears that we will be dining with our friends after all.

When they entered the diner. Charlie and Brenda were at a booth setting next to each other making it convenient for Marla and Brett to slide into the booth across from them.

"Hey guys, mind if we join you?" Marla asked.

"Course not, we actually thought about calling you, but we figured you were busy house hunting." Charlie said.

"As a matter of fact, Charlie, we called the Patterson's to invite you to dine with us. They told us you were at the diner, but we had no idea you were at Frank's, anyway the results are the same and we're here together in spite of everything, nice to see you Brenda. You notice I didn't address Charlie but then I see him every day.

"That's okay Brett, it's good to see you both back. I think we should do it more often. How's house hunting going?" He asked.

"Well Charlie, we made an offer, will find out tomorrow morning, but I have a feeling we're going to have a deal. We want both of you to have a tour if you would like to go with us in the morning. Charlie's house is better than the one we live in Marla. He has three bedrooms, two baths where I have only one. Perhaps he was looking to the future when he bought his place."

"Sounds like a plan, Brett, four bedrooms and three bathrooms, that's a lot of space to fill. You must be planning on having a Little League of kids."

"Whoa, nobody said anything about kids, in fact, we have never discussed having kids, were not even engaged and I wouldn't have any children unless we decide to wed." Brett said, setting them straight on the subject of children.

Brett asked, "When are you and Brenda planning on moving forward together?" You could see their faces turning red as a beet.

"Well, although we are close, I don't think Brenda is at that part of our relationship just yet, I'm going to take her by my house after dinner. She's never seen where I live yet, I guess that's all right honey?" Charlie asked. I think he was kind of pushed into that vibrant statement.

"If you need to know, we have discussed that very subject and it's still under consideration."

"Well, Charlie it all depends on whether you love her or not, or likely won't work if you don't for Marla me, we knew you immediately and it's really great. I can't imagine not having her in my life and by my side as well. Just like you, two waiting to get back together, big mistake. Just look at all the things you've missed out on."

"Sometimes you make good sense Brett, I guess that's why you're so good at what you do I mean, by running a great business. Maybe I will become the CEO there or perhaps the straw boss someday." Charlie said sincerely.

They had a great dinner and a ton of conversation; Brenda didn't have much to say but for sure she was taking it all in.

They shared another glass of wine; Brett left a nice tip and left the diner in separate vehicles.

Brett and Marla went straight home, it was 10:30 not too late but they had some talking to do to prepare for Sunday, expecting a phone call by 10:00 AM.

They went into the living room for a glass of wine and turned on the TV. There was an official making an announcement not about this bank robbery, it was more of a plea to the public soliciting help to anyone that is new about the robbers anything they could remember no matter how insignificant it might seem to them. It could be of help catching the bandits before they struck again.

"You think they're ever going to catch them babe, I mean, how long has it been since the last robbery?"

"I don't know the answers to your questions, don't know when the last robbery was. I can remember but it was approximately just a day or two before Labor Day. Brenda and I were on a trip on the

Labor Day weekend at Pine Cove, you knew we discovered a woman's body, didn't you?"

"No, you never mentioned it to me. How did that come about?"

"Well like I said Brenda and I were on vacation on the Labor Day weekend. That's where we met the cowboys, they showed us how to fish, we also went swimming off of the dock. Anyhow, you wouldn't be interested in how we met the cowboys. I suggested to Brenda after packing the SUV that we needed the exercise. We had not done much walking or hiking as of exercise, so I suggested to Brenda that we take a hike. We started walking up the mountainside. We flagged the trees so we wouldn't get lost coming back, anyway, we walked about 100 yards. That's about a football field in distance suddenly we came upon a woman's body, we stayed back and made mental notes, when we got back to the rest area which was about an hour's drive towards home there happened to be a phone booth and I called the Police Department and gave them all the data in detail including making the trail so we didn't destroy any evidence. I took off my blouse and ripped it up in little pieces and hung it on the trees on our way back so hopefully the police could find their way up without us marking the trip back again."

"Wow, I heard about the robbery, but they never mentioned you and Brenda on the news. I suppose they were protecting your names. I suppose it makes you famous."

"No, that makes this unfortunate. It was very shocking. Although we are used to death. We see it all as I'm at the hospital. However, we know it's happening, which is different than stumbling onto a dead person, I didn't sleep for three days."

Brett put his arms around her, she put her hand on his shoulder. They remain silent for a few minutes.

"Let's go to bed sweetheart, we have a busy day tomorrow."

The two lovebirds retired for the evening, cuddled up and with the tender kiss and a good night and they fell asleep.

The sun found its way through an opening in the drapes waking Marla, she turned facing Brett she kissed him on the tip of his nose, "Time to get up dude," she said.

"I thought we were going to sleep in on Sunday morning. What's up, and What time is it?" He asked.

"7 o'clock," she answered.

"So, why are we getting up so early?"

"Because you have a phone call supposedly at 10 o'clock this morning, don't you remember?"

"Yeah, that's right. We have a house to buy this a.m., so let's hit the shower and grab something to eat at home, don't know if there's enough time to eat out."

"Let's take care of first things first," Brett got excited. He thought she was talking about something else. "You lay there while I shower, and I'll fix breakfast for you while you're getting ready, how's that? And what about pancakes and a couple scrambled eggs?"

"Sounds great, can I do anything to help? He asked.

"No, just stay in bed and let me get showered and dressed. I think everything will go much smoother."

She hit the shower and he hit the pillow, soon she came into the room to get dressed and found that Brett had dozed off.

"Okay, cowboy, get yourself out of bed and into the shower, soon as I get dressed, I'll see you in the kitchen."

He did as she requested. Soon the aroma of fresh coffee filled the room. Brett came into the kitchen, grabbed Marla around the waist, turned her around and they kissed fervently.

She said," if we keep this up here we will end up in the bedroom and we don't have time for that."

"Oh, come on, a little kiss won't do any harm, and besides, we're waiting for a 10 o'clock phone call so there'll be no playing around this morning." He said, wishing it wasn't true.

Do you think she will call at 10 o'clock?" She questioned.

"No, Brett answered," she will linger for 15 or 20 minutes. Like she's not totally interested in expecting me to up the ante, but I shall remain firm." He declared.

"Have a seat honey. Breakfast is almost ready." Marla said.

9:15 The phone rang, "I can't believe it, maybe I misunderstood her." Brett picked up the phone to his surprise of a different kind, it was Brenda, she said," Charlie and I would like to go with you to look at the house. Can we come over there, leave our car and ride with you?"

"Of course, that's a great idea. You surprised me. I thought the call was from the agent but then it's still early. Come over when you're ready." Brett said as he hung up the phone

"Who was that Brett, was it the agent? I thought you said she would be lingering around and wouldn't call early, taking her time."

"Nope, it was Brenda. She and Charlie they're on their way here they're going with us isn't that great?"

Marla had just finished washing the dishes when the doorbell rang, it was Charlie and Brenda." Are we ready to go?" Charlie asked.

"Not yet, still waiting for the agent to call, she's due in the next half hour, let's have a seat in the living room, anyone for coffee?" Brett asked.

They declined the offer for coffee, but they did take a seat in the living room and started a conversation about the new house and whether or not they would buy it.

"Oh," Brett said, "if if I get the price I offered, I will be buying a house. I've been waiting to get more room for a long time and the time has finally arrived."

It wasn't long before the call they were waiting for came, just before 10:30 but will it be what Brett wanted to hear?

The agent said, "Good morning Mr. Conklin, the owner said if you would come back with the original offer of $300,000 they would let the house go."

Brett returned with, "Give me 30 minutes to talk it over with my fiancé and I can call you with hopefully an answer, perhaps we can reach a mutual compromise."

At that. They said their goodbyes and hung up the phone.

"Well guys were getting close, they counted with $300,000 only $5,000 more than I offered. What you say Marla sounds good enough or should we stay firm and take a chance on losing the house. I guess I can always give them what they're asking."

"This sounds to me like you've already made up your mind. Why don't we accept this offer? It's only $5,000, if we can offer $295,000. I'm sure the $5,000 is good enough and it won't Break us one way or the other."

"Okay sweetheart, make the call."

Brett called the agent and told her they would like to come talk to her at her office and close the deal, "However we would like to walk through it once more. Can you meet us at the property in 30 minutes?"

The Agent agreed, so the four of them climbed into Brett's car and drove away to show Charlie and Brenda their soon to be new prized possession, maybe this will spark some new life into their plans to move in together. It would be great if they were totally together. They could all have fun, enjoy backyard barbecues and even spend some nights together. I think it's about time Brett moves his relationship forward, and maybe gets down on one knee, it's looking good.

When they arrived at their destination. The agent was just going through the gate, she stopped making sure Brett could get it before the gate closed.

"Well, here we are, guys," Brett said as he pulled up in front of the house.

"Looks beautiful,Brett," Brenda said, "I can't wait to see inside. I bet it's really beautiful."

"Well, for one who's been inside I'd say you're right it is beautiful," Marla added.

"Have you been to Charlie's house, Brenda?, it's really nice but an older house and I don't mean that as a punch in the ribs. Charlie, I'm dead serious." Brett said.

"No," Brenda said, "Charlie has never misguided me yet," I think she just opened Pandora's box.

"Well, sweetheart, confident the deal was done the next time we go to breakfast or dinner I'll take you there. I think you're going to like what you see." Charlie concluded.

They went inside and it was everything it was said to be.

"Oh Marla, this is truly beautiful. Maybe one day Charlie and…" she stopped short of adding her name to the sentence. Her face turned red as a beet.

Charlie, noticing her complexion, took her hand and said, "Don't be embarrassed sweetheart. It's been my plan for a long time, but when you come to visit my present house. I'm sure you will agree it's nice. It has three bedrooms, two baths, and of course the kitchen and living room, and the dining room is quite spacious."

"I believe you Charlie we would someday live like Marla and Brett; hope I'm not jumping the gun." She said apologetically.

"I sure hope so love, I've been looking forward to our moving forward with her relationship, and the sooner the better."

"Do you think your folks will throw monkey wrench into our plans, I mean, I know how they expect you to live your life but moving in with me without being arbitrarily married I just don't know." Charlie said.

"Don't worry Hon, just because I'm an only child, doesn't mean I have to live with the family forever. I mean, I know they expect me to move out at some point in time."

"That's right Brenda, I'm sure they expect you to move out at some time in your life, it's not like you're a teenager."

"Well, let's move onto a different subject, like when are you going to show me your house?" She questioned being very sensitive about the subject.

"How about tomorrow?" Charlie asked.

"Do you mean to see the house or to move in? I don't know about you, but I have to work." She laughed.

"Oh, that's right, he replied, tomorrow is Monday, isn't it?"

"It sure is. But, perhaps sometime soon, no big rush."

"I've got an idea, let's go to dinner after work tomorrow and will go to my place afterwards? What do you say Brenda?"

"Sounds great, Charlie. We can kill two birds with one stone, have dinner and see your place at the same time."

"Okay Charlie said, it's a deal."

They went home to Brenda's house. It was still early so Charlie went inside and had a glass of wine with Mr. Patterson. They were talking about his plans for the future, especially where his daughter was involved.

It kind of took Charlie by surprise. He now wished he had kept going instead of stopping by the house. But he backed himself into a corner and had to come up with some sort of a solution. Before he could ask Mr. Patterson the question Brenda walked into the room with a glass of wine, "What are you two talking about, me?" She asked.

Mr. Patterson spoke up, "As a matter of fact we were, and Charlie was about to answer my question right, Charlie?" Talk about being backed into a corner.

He took Brenda by the hand, saying, "Well, Mr. Patterson, I plan to one day to marry your daughter if she'll have me, however, is not on the calendar just yet, in fact, we haven't an even had the opportunity to talk about it, but it's definitely been on my mind. However, I would've preferred to ask and get down on one knee at a different time and location. I have a question, when I asked for her hand in marriage will I have your blessings?" Charlie asked with his eye on Mr. Patterson.

"We'll see what happens." He returned, "However my daughter is old enough to make up her own mind. I think the world of you Charlie and I believe you would make a great addition to the family, so you two go on with your life and will see how it works out." At that, he concluded his statement.

It was getting past Mr. Patterson's bedtime; Charlie took Brenda by the hand asking her to walk him out. She of course was willing to do so.

Outside they stood on the porch and embraced. Charlie said, "I'm in love with you Brenda, I hope that you can one day love me as much."

"I've been waiting to hear those words. I've been in love with you from the second day we met."

Charlie said, I was afraid of rejection but I'm glad I finally got the guts to say the words and knowing that you love me too, will make it easy to say the words I held back for so long, I'm so relieved."

"I had better go into the house. Things are getting a little heated and we would want to do anything to spoil our relationship, now would we?" She questioned.

Charlie was a little with her statement he thought they just said they loved each other; what could we possibly do spoil our relationship. That was only minutes ago when they confirmed their love for each other. He wondered; However, he would respect her wish. One final kiss and one question, "Have I done something wrong, if so, I apologize."

"Not at all. I was referring to a solution of a sexual nature, and I sure wouldn't want to do anything stupid here on the porch." She replied.

That statement gave Charlie a feeling of optimism, he said, "I'm still sorry, some other place, another time." He said.

"We'll see Charlie, but I must say, it looks promising." With that she kissed him lightly on the lips, said good night and entered the house.

Charlie drove away so happy he was whistling; God save the King. (Not really.)

It was a heck of a strain on Charlie as well and I'm sure she knew it. Perhaps things will be more formidable, when they stay at his house. He planned on taking her to dinner tomorrow night before the tour of Brett's new house. He was amazed how Brett got close to Marla and look how they turned out. Charlie hoped it would work the same for him and Brenda. He's not sure if she will move in or not but he fully intends to give the old college a try.

Brenda met Marla at the hospital, there were standing at the nurses desk when Brenda said, "Charlie and I almost had sex on the front porch of my house last night, well not really sex but the thought was in the back of our mind's I had to push him away and go into the house before we did something wrong."

"It isn't wrong Brenda, just the wrong place at the wrong time. What you must do is follow your heart and give into your feelings. we gave up our life only so we could finish college and do the job well. Like we're doing now. But we gave up a lot, it's been a long time since we've enjoyed the life we're living now, and we still have our jobs, so I'd say we've accomplished our goals."

"Well Marla, I think Charlie and I are going to dinner tonight after work. After that he's taking me to see the house. I'm afraid I don't know his intentions, what would you do if you were me?"

"Okay Brenda, like I said follow your heart and have no regrets, I did. I spent the night now quit being afraid of letting yourself go. I promise you if you two have the same feelings for each other as Brett I did. You will be happy, A camper, that's a promise."

"You really don't mind throwing in the towel and giving in after our realm not to get too involved until we've finished college, became nurses, and we have no regrets? We finished college seven years ago and followed our dreams, nursing, you're so right. I guess it's time to enjoy life again." She hugged Marla and thanked her. She turned and walked away. She remained in a daze for the rest of the day, anxious for her shift to end so she could meet Charlie and see where it takes them.

She later asked," would you and Brett like to go to Charlie's with us tonight, you haven't seen his house either?" Sounds like Brenda's confidence was at an all-time low.

"Brenda, we've been friends forever as much as I would like to see Charlie's house, and I'm sure I will eventually, but you need to do this one on your own, my being there would only delay the inevitable."

"I guess you're right Marla, it's time for me to grow up and do what's expected of me. I love Charlie and he loves me so why am I afraid, I have to come out of my shell sometime, might as well be tonight."

Marla hugged Brenda after work in the parking lot, "Good luck Brenda. I'm confident you'll be just fine."

Marla wound her hand around the wheel of a car, said a word to Brenda and drove away.

She got home at 6:15 PM, 45 minutes before Brett usually leaves work. Marla started preparing for her and Brett. She thought she would surprise him by having dinner ready by the time he walks through the door. Brett pulled into the driveway at six forty-five 15 minutes earlier than usual. When he opened the door, he made sure there was no surprise awaiting him, "Okay Marla, where are you, not hiding are you?" "If you call cooking hiding, then I guess I am."

CHAPTER 10

NO SURPRISES HERE

Brett turned the corner into the kitchen, no surprises there she was slaving over a hot stove next to a bowl of salad.

"Sit, I'll pour you a glass of wine." She ordered.

"I see you got a head start." He returned noticing a half empty glass in front of her.

"Well, one never knows what time her possible husband might pop in, so I just poured myself a glass. You can see I still have most of it left. I was waiting for you, and didn't want to get too far ahead. Do you like roast beef, mashed potatoes and gravy?" She asked.

"Yeah, I love all of them, are they going to be ready soon?"

"Yes, I'm glad you love roast beef, however having pork roast instead of beef."

"That's fine. I like them both." He really didn't care much for pork. However, he would eat whatever she cooked making sure she thought he enjoyed it.

Brett said the island across from where she was. A mixed green salad.

"Is it almost done, Hon, it's not that I'm starving. I just miss your company on the other side of the island." He commented.

"I'll tell you what, I'll clear the island and we can sit next to each other and have dinner at the same time, what do you say?" She asked, wearing a smile.

Marla served dinner and took a seat to the left side of Brett. He put his hand on hers with her palm down on the island, she said, "I don't think I can eat with my left hand and you have my right hand pinned down on the counter top."

"I'm sorry, he said, I just can't seem to keep my hands off of you."

"That's right, sweetheart. I feel the same, but we had better eat before it gets cold. We can do all the touching we want after dinner."

"That sounds inviting, but that wasn't what I meant I just love your touch. That's sweet babe, but your dinner is getting cold. We'll talk about it after we finish dinner. You wouldn't have me spending hours in a hot kitchen and let the food goes cold, would you?"

"When are we going to start moving into our new house or is it too early to go forward?" She asked.

Well, kind of, we haven't signed a contract yet, but I think that will be history in a day or two. You can always start putting your things together at least you will have a head start."

After dinner they watch TV for about an hour before retiring, "We need sleep If you're going to work tomorrow and I You know you are."

"How about your plan on staying home, I'm only asking because you said, we." She questioned with a slight laugh.

He showered the next morning and Brett kissed Marla saying, "I'll see you tonight babe."

"Okay, do you want me to start dinner or do you have other plans?" She asked.

"No, not really, although we could go to Frank's for dinner. Foods are good and they Fix it the way you want it, and you won't have to cook."

"Good idea, I'll be showered, dressed and ready to go when you get home."

"Sounds good, see you tonight." Brett said as he walked out the door.

Charlie pulled into the parking lot just before Brett. He was wearing a broad smile.

"What are you so happy about this morning Charlie?" Brett asked.

"Does it show? Brenda and I spent the night at my house last night, looks like she's moving in with me." He answered.

"Well, that's enough to bring a smile to a crocodile. Brett said" life is about to take a change for the better. I know mine sure did after Marla and I moved in together." Oh, by the way Marla and I are eating dinner at Frank's, why don't you two join us. I'm buying." He concluded.

On their way into the office they met Justin heading towards the rear of the building where he would spend his day putting computer parts together.

"Are you ready for the day Justin?" Brett asked.

"Yeah, I'm as ready as I'm gonna get, kind of anxious to get started." He said, returning Brett's question.

Brett went into the office, Charlie headed to the rear of the building with Justin, one of Charlie's jobs to make sure Justin didn't make mistakes. His primary job was parts. He would advance to more critical jobs like airplane computer parts that is when he proves he could handle them; everybody has to start somewhere and that's usually at the beginning.

At noon, Brett invited Justin and Charlie to lunch, nobody turns down a free lunch, if There is such a thing.

Next thing you know, the day was over, Brett reminded Charlie about dinner at Frank's, they said goodbye and took off in different directions.

When Brett got home, Marla was just as she said she would be ready to go out the door, well almost, no matter when you think a woman is ready, they always have to put on some extra makeup that kills another 20 minutes. That's all right, He loves her.

He gave her a kiss and told her about Brenda and Charlie moving in together. Marla was surprised it happened so fast.

Brett said, "Isn't that great, Oh, and they're having dinner with us so we'd better get going, I'll be ready in 20 minutes. Pour us a glass of wine, okay sweetheart?"

"Okay but hurry we wouldn't want to be late. It's going to be interesting watching them squirm." She said jokingly.

Brett was ready in 20 minutes, he walked into the kitchen drinking wine, which was only about 2 ounces, Marla made sure they would be on time.

Marla and Brett pulled into Frank's surprise as Charlie's car had yet to show up, but Brett was sure he would be there in a few minutes. I guess they had time to drink their wine after all.

They went into the restaurant, took a booth near the window and ordered a glass of wine and waited for Charlie and Brenda's arrival.

Soon the happy couple came Strutting through the door with their hands locked, like one might get away.

When Marla saw them coming through the door. She got up and moved next to Brett so Charlie and Brenda could sit side-by-side.

They, Charlie and Brenda, were wearing a broad smile. They are about to join the lovers club.

"How are you doing girl?" Marla asked. "You're looking happy."

"Great," she returned, acting a little Gaudi." I'll tell you all about it at work tomorrow." Brenda said.

They each ordered a round of wine while scanning through the menu. Brett and Marla ordered the same thing: steak with baked potato and all the trimmings and a green salad.

Charlie and Brenda had roast beef with mashed potatoes and gravy, also with a green salad.

They talked about everything from work to vacations. Girls are eligible for two weeks' vacation. They can take them almost anytime they choose, as long as it fits into their schedule.

Brett, on the other hand, owns a business, he can take off anytime. However, he won't leave if there's any account pending.

"How's Justin working out Charlie, think he'll ever learn, so far, I'm everything negative about him." Brett commented.

"Well it's still early Brett, I think he'll make it okay. He's pretty good with his hands and his brain as well."

"How about we have a barbecue at our new house, say the week after Saturday comes. We should have our new furniture in place by then."

"You're buying new furniture Brett, what's wrong with the furniture you have?" Question Brenda.

"Because we're going to rent the old house, I mean it's paid for So, whatever we take in as rent is money in our pockets." Brett explained.

"Good thinking" Charlie said, "It seems you have everything worked out."

"Yeah, Marla stepped in, "it's about houses and furniture we'll give the two of you an update. The words going around that you Two moved in together any truth to that rumor?" Marla asked, putting Brenda into a situation. Kind of like being backed into a corner and no way out.

Brenda's face turned red, she was so embarrassed, but she had to confirm or deny no other choice except silence, "Yes we did. I was so surprised Charlie asked me to move in with him but, knowing how happy you and Brett are. I guess if it works for you, we might as well give it a try." (Good explanation Brenda.)

"Well Brenda, you already have that glow about you and don't worry it will work out just fine, wait-and-see." Marla concludes her statement.

"Is it your intention to embarrass me Marla, if so, it's working." Brenda said, still wearing rosy cheeks.

"Not at all, girl. I'm so glad you two finally came together. You'll make a beautiful couple and I hope one day if everything progresses, we may have a double wedding."

"Wow, I never saw that coming, but the idea sounds great to me, but I think the news should come from the men." Brenda said.

"Yeah," Charlie said, "we haven't discussed any engagement plans yet, but I hope it will happen soon."

When they finished their dinner. They said their good nights and drove off in separate directions, Brenda felt she had some explaining to do with her family, after all, this was totally unexpected

They pulled up in the driveway in front of the Patterson's, Charlie got out, went around and opened the door for Brenda. Hand in hand they entered the house, "Mom, dad, let us go into the living room." They sat down on the couch, expecting that perhaps their daughter was about to make an announcement. It was their engagement and they weren't ready for what was about to happen or what Patterson was about to hear.

"Well, you may or may not like what I'm about to say, but here goes," Charlie was holding her hand when she spoke, "Charlie and I are moving in together, just to see how compatible we are and if things work out and I'm sure they will. We will get engaged, and in the future get married. What do you think about that?" She questioned expecting rejection.

"Well, her father said, you know we're against people living together without being married, however, we also know we have no control over your life, after all, you're more than old enough and capable of making your own decisions."

"Will you get by all right without my tiny denotation, like paying some of the bills? You think you can handle it on your own. I know you're not poor, but I've always helped in a small fashion and I'd feel guilty if I don't continue?"

"Well now, don't you worry about that Brenda I fully intended to totally support you whatever your contribution is, I'm sure we can handle it on our own. I don't plan on you dipping into your pension or account, it's yours. You earned every penny of it and you can do with it of your own choosing." He concluded.

"That goes for me as well Charlie' just because it's my money and I earned it but as long as we are going to partner up, we should share everything, the good and the bad." Brenda explained.

Discussions went on for a half-hour until she said, "I guess we had better go, don't you think sweetheart?"

"Yes," he replied "I think we've accomplished our mission. Let's go home and contemplate tomorrow, what do you say?"

Marla and Brett pulled up in front of their house, "let's go to bed early and discuss the future," he suggested.

"Sounds great, Brett. I am kinda tired anyhow, it's been a long day for both of us and we have to discuss when we are going to make the move to our beautiful new residence. Saturday the furniture will be delivered to the new house. We need to be there when the furniture arrives so we can make sure it's properly located. We want to make sure everything is in the right place."

"Shall we invite Charlie and Brenda, who knows they may have some suggestions we're overlooking?"

Marla called Brenda the next morning and asked if she and Charlie would be interested in helping them with the location of the furniture. "You think you might be bored?"

"No, I'm sure Charlie will be elated just being involved in your new adventure."

"Okay, I will give you a call when we are ready to go. We have a ton of packing to do before we move in completely, probably some of the time we might even have a little entertainment next weekend perhaps have a BBQ, will play it by ear."

"Do you mean like you play the piano?" Brenda chuckled.

"No silly, if the move goes as badly as when I play the piano. We never will get moved." Marla said, setting the record straight.

Brett engaged in the conversation, "I didn't know you played the piano sweetheart, will have to include one with the furniture."

"That's a great offer my dear, but you don't just order a piano, you must shop for one, and test it out otherwise you wouldn't know if you were getting a good sounding one, besides, they're very expensive. I'm not sure we're ready for one until we move in."

Saturday morning, the four gathered at Brett's house, they planned to help in every way together to help them get moved in. There will be movers going in and out of the house all day long.

Brett decided they should wait until after 4 o'clock and not get into their way. Unbeknownst to the rest of them Brett had added bottles of good wine to be put in the refrigerator to chill, looks like a little celebration might ensue. In the meantime, Brett offered to take everyone to breakfast since they were nice enough to help with the move. "Where would you like to go for breakfast? Anyone, just name it and we're off and running." Brett said.

"Well," Brenda said, "there's always Frank's, but then we spend a lot of our time there, maybe we should try something a little different for change. You remember that little popular café in the middle of town?"

"Yeah," Brett responded, "you mean the one we had to stand in line forever, just to get to the door, yeah, I remember and the only reason I would give it a second thought is because the food was so good. So yeah, let's do it If it's all right with Brenda and Charlie."

They all agreed on the little restaurant nobody remembered the name of in the middle of downtown Pleasantville.

The group arrived at the restaurant at 10 o'clock sharp, they were sitting down to eat at 10:45, the restaurant shuts down at 11:00 for breakfast I guess to prepare for lunch.

Well as luck would have it, they made it by 10:45 so it looks like they're in for breakfast.

During breakfast most of the conversation was about how well they paired up and how much love was in the air. When it was about love, conversation would turn to the excitement of visiting Brett's new house.

After breakfast they drove around the city in the area of the house, he purchased just in the event that neither Brenda nor Charlie had ever seen the area. Most of the homes are in gated communities. They drove around so long it was time for lunch and so they had lunch. They still had time to kill, so they went to the park. There was a little pond in the center of the park, they enjoyed themselves by feeding the ducks, sounds boring to me, but whatever floats your boat.

Finally, 4:15, rolled around, it was time to look at the new house and make changes in the furniture and if necessary, deletion or locations.

Marla was the first to say, "Oh Brett, it's beautiful, and you picked out all this furniture yourself, you're amazing."

Charlie and Brenda chimed in, "Wow it is really beautiful. Brett, when are you moving in?"

"Don't know for sure but soon, Marla is in the process of packing now. So, it won't be long." Brett explained.

"C'mon on Brenda let's look at the kitchen." Marla said. "Charlie lets you and I have a look at the living room."

"Oh my God Brett," Charlie said amazed, "How big is that TV taking up the whole wall."

"Oh, you noticed huh. It's 80 inches. Pretty neat, wouldn't you say Charlie?"

"Boy, I'd say so, can't wait for football season, we can have a barbecue in the backyard and watch our favorite games on that large-screen."

"I'm not sure if Marla would appreciate company every weekend, you know she enjoys other things besides football. I think shopping at the mall is her thing, not mine."

"I didn't mean to imply that Brenda and I would be intruding every week, only when our favorite teams are playing If it's alright with you."

"I know Charlie, I'm just jerking your chain, I'm sure Marla and Brenda would prefer going shopping anyway."

"I doubt it. I don't speak for Brenda, but I'm sure Marla would rather shop while we sat around drinking wine and utilizing that humongous TV."

"Well now, that you put it that way. I think you're probably right." Brett said as the two men went into the kitchen where the ladies were discussing something over a glass of wine.

"Well, that's nice," Brett said, expressing his feelings, "how come you didn't call us thirsty too, and how did you know that I ordered wine to be put into the refrigerator just for this special occasion. At least there are two of you partying."

They all gathered around the living room, Brenda noticed the TVs she'd never seen one that large. "Wow Brett, that's not a TV. It looks more like a movie screen, I bet Charlie can't wait for football season?"

"You're right Brenda. Those were his exact words and you're both invited any time. We'll have to have you over once in a while, right Marla?"

They sat in the living room drinking wine and watching a movie on the big screen. Charlie said, "This is a lot of fun guys, but we have to work tomorrow so I guess we better break it up Brenda and go home, get some rest."

Everyone agreed and the party broke up. They locked up the house and all climbed into Brett's car and headed for Brett's and

Marla's house to pick up Charlie's car. For he and Brenda this will be the third night together, so far everything is hunky-dory.

Finally, Brett and Marla were home. "As much as you like your friends sometimes, they can be too much, especially when you want solitude." Brett stated.

The night went as it should have gone when two people love each other, enjoy the night tomorrow will be here before you know it.

Monday was the same old grind, Brett went in one direction and Marla and the other, of course, Marla had a little more time than Brett. She didn't have to be at work until 9 AM. Without having to pick up Brenda after realizing she no longer lived with her parents. However, the two met in the hall and walked together to the nurse's station chatting about Marla's new house, and how fortunate she was to run into Brett at the store. Had she not, she may still be lonesome for who knows how long.?

Marla's shift went well, fortunately, the hospital didn't have the usual weekend traffic, although there were a few that had the problem of too much to drink and fighting in the war of denial, it was just another weekend in Pleasantville.

Marla said goodbye to Brenda out in the parking lot and left heading home to start dinner for Brett and her. She wanted to do the cooking herself. They spent too much time eating out, besides, she loved surprising Brett with her menu.

She stops at the market on the way home and picked up some beef, potatoes, celery, and whatever it takes to make beef stew, now the question is does she have time to make it before Brett arrived home, probably not however, shopping included two bottles of wine that would hold them over until after dinner.

Brett walked into the house about 7:30. "Smells good, what have you got cooking?"

"Beef stew, however, we may have to wait for a while. I'll pour the wine and will sit in the living room until it's ready, okay?" she questioned.

They walked into the living room, each carrying a glass of wine. They took a seat next to each other on the divan and began a conversation.... Marla suggested that he turn on the television. "We haven't watched the news much recently."

"Yeah, it's probably the same old things, a DUI with hit-and-run cars crashing all over the place, same old same old."

Just as the TV came on it started with, as I said before, at 10 o'clock this morning Just as the bank was opening for business. A bandit walked up behind the few people waiting for the door to open, they were forced in at gunpoint and a threat. Inside the patrons were ordered to get face down on the floor, most cooperated. It was a single man dressed as a same person as the tallest male of the two men who robbed the same bank two years ago. The only good witness was recuperating in the hospital with a bullet in her stomach. The doctor said that she was in a coma and may not awaken for at least a week, but she was otherwise stable.

I guess the FBI is going to have to give this robber some time to escape to another state. Given the time the witness might be out. That could be 3 to 4 days or even longer he can travel halfway across the states in that link of time.

The FBI started their investigation, went through the same old routine, talking to all the witnesses and the guard who was not only face down on the floor and forced to push his gun away from them deeming him powerless to do anything but obey. Must be a weird feeling having that authority and can't use it.

Just before the bandit was in and out the door in less than a minute, how the witness was able to see the man when nobody else did remains a mystery, at least for some time.

The only difference in this robbery was the shorter man wasn't present and the taller of the two didn't wear a hoodie just to a bear face as if he wanted to get caught.

"Well Frank, the Senior agent said, we should get a pretty good ID on this creep as soon as the lady awakens, if she does."

"Yeah, and we might as well head in and we've done all that we can do here."

"Okay Frank, what you say we stop by the hospital just in case we get lucky?"

"Yeah, fat chance, but nothing ventured, nothing gained."

They drove away continuing the robbery conversation and hoping for the best. "If we only had a picture of this dude, we could send it out on TV and other social media. But without a good identification will be wasting everybody's time."

They stopped by the hospital and went directly to the nurse's station to inquire about the possible witness. The nurse told him her room number, but that they couldn't enter because the patient was still in a coma.

The officers thanked the nurse turned and walked away. One of them commented, "He's probably on a plane to Zanzibar by now."

"Do you really think he would go so far as Zanzibar?" The detective questioned.

"It was a joke, Al just a joke. Come on, let's get out of here." Detective Frank was shaking his head as they entered the parking lot.

Marla asked Brenda, the next day. "Did you see the news last night, I bet we ran into those two detectives in the hallway this morning but probably not?" She said just shaking it off.

The day came to an end, Marla and Brenda walked out of the hospital together. "What would you say if we stop on the way home and have a drink? Our guys won't be home until at least 7:30. I know I'd call Brett and have them meet us. What do you call your game?" Marla asked.

"Because we haven't been to Frank's for a while, this time we will sit at the bar?" Brenda returned.

Marla answered with one word, "deal."

They parked the car behind Franks and entered through the rear door, not supposed to, but Brenda was pretty sure they would get away with it Marla said, "Let's have something besides wine. What was that you fixed me the first time I had a drink?"

"I'm not sure it's been a while; I think it was Margarita. You remember we made a joke about ordering a topless Maggie?"

The girls were on their second drink when Brett and Charlie came walking through the door, and I might add a bit disturbed that the girls were sitting at the bar. I think they expected to find them at the booth. Setting it a bar sometimes indicates you want to pick somebody up, but they were not.

Brett took a seat to the right of Marla while Charlie sat on the left side of Brenda.

"What's going on, girls. I thought you had come in here to eat, but it looks like you're going to get drunk instead, what's up?" Brett questioned.

"You're being a bit harsh there Brett, we just wanted something other than wine. That's all, as for getting drunk. I would never want to do that again I'm sorry if you truly feel that way." Marla said she was serious, and Brett knew it, he began to sweat, hoping this would not end up in a breakup.

"I'm sorry sweetheart I'm weighing too much into this, just surprised I guess, what the hell let's party. We can always take a cab home."

"Will you two ladies be able to nurse with a hangover?" Brett snickered.

"We don't know we've never gone to work with a hangover." Marla said.

"I guess we'll have to wait and see what happens, however, when the alarm goes off at 7 AM. Be prepared to get your Tish, get out of bed and hit the shower. You cannot afford to be late or miss a shift. Although I'm not sure what the hospital rules are, there could be two strikes and you're out. Maybe they have special rules for certain nurses that have been there for a long period of time, like you we'll find out."

"What makes you so certain we're going to get drunk, is not our first drink you know." Marla said, getting a little angry.

"You're right sweetheart, it's not the first drink that gets you, it's the last one." He said with a snicker.

"Oh Brett, you're so smart. You know I don't want to get drunk. The last time I did you took advantage of me." She declared.

"I did not, all I did was undress you and put you into bed. I waited until the next night so you could say I took advantage of you, and you loved it. He said with a broad smile.

"Yeah, and I suppose you didn't, right?" She ended with laughter.

Brenda spoke, "You two are putting out way too much information, but it is funny."

"Was it as funny as your first night after all the years we remained celibate?"

Brett let the girls go ahead and get it out of their system. He held back so they could take care of Marla, Charlie knew that was true so he slowed down drinking so he could care for Brenda, they didn't know at that moment, but tomorrow the girls would be more appreciative than they knew at the time.

Meanwhile the girls kept slipping down the margaritas I guess they were waiting to see which one would fall first.

About 12 o'clock, both girls were slurring through their words and it didn't go unnoticed, Brett said, "Okay girls, it's time to go." There was minor resistance, but it didn't last long.

Brett helped Marla off the stool and headed towards the rear door ricocheting from one table to the other. I know he wasn't thinking too kindly about the situation, but he kept to himself.

Charlie attempted to help Brenda, but she put up some resistance, saying, "I don't need your help." She insisted. He walked alongside her, almost hitting the floor and taking him down with her. Well it didn't make him very happy; he pulled her next to him and put his arms around her shoulders.

With the girls safely tucked away in the cars. Charlie said, "some night huh, Brett, and we didn't even have dinner."

"Yeah, I will take care of that after I put Marla into bed."

Charlie laughed as he drove away. His night wasn't over, yet he still had to put Brenda to bed, he'll sleep in the other bedroom tonight.

When Brett finally got home and put Marla to bed, after dragging her through the living room to the bedroom. He would sleep on the couch with an attitude, everybody has one.

Morning came, Marla was snoring like a bear in hibernation. Brett was already in the shower contemplating whether or not to wake Marla who was sound asleep. Brett was hesitant to wake her, but it was a necessity that could not be denied. He shook her on the shoulder.

"What you want, get out of here and let me sleep. I have a horrible headache" She said in a nasty tone of voice.

"Hit the shower, you're going to be late for work, you are going to work are you not? He asked in a loud enough voice to get her attention.

After a short battle of words. She jumped out of bed and ran to the shower, holding her head.

Brett decided to go to work a little late to make sure she would make her shift on time.

CHAPTER 11

A LITTLE HAIR OFF THE DOG

30 minutes passed; Marla showed up in the kitchen surprised that Brett was still at home. He usually goes to work a half-hour before she does.

He asked, "What are you doing at home aren't you going to work? I have a headache that a full bottle of aspirin won't cure."

"I promise I won't say I told you so," he said, "here drink this it works faster than a bottle of aspirin."

"What is it she questioned?"

"A bloody Mary or as we drunks call it "The hair of the dog." he snickered.

"I don't want anything with alcohol, is there really a hair of the dog in it?"

"Drink it and I guarantee you there is no hair, but you feel better in minutes that I promise there is no hair in it. However, don't kiss any doctors or get too close to other nurses."

Marla took a sip and spit it out, that anger Brett all he was trying to do was help get her back on her feet, he put the glass to her lips, "Drink it down it won't help the sink. It doesn't usually need help. Now please drink it. I can leave for work until you do so please swallow it down."

She made a face, he kissed her on the lips and said "I'll meet you at Frank's tonight." I think he was joking.

She made a nasty remark as he passed through the door.

Marla and Brenda met in the hospital parking lot and walked through the hall together. Brenda looked even worse than Marla, but then she probably didn't have a bloody Mary to start her day.

"How come you Fanny isn't Dragging, mine sure is. I guess I won't be stopping at Frank's or any other bar for a while. Brenda said addressing.

Marla, who looked calm and refreshed.

"Brenda, did Charlie fix you a bloody Mary before you left for work this morning, I thought I would surely die until Brett made me drink one I never thought I'd see the day I'd have a drink that early in the morning. I don't know anything in the hospital that can help you, not even if there was a building full of drunks." Marla said with a slight snickered.

"Meet me in the locker room and I'll get something for your woozy head." Marla said like a drill sergeant.

She left and headed for the locker room and waited for Marla to show up with her surprise, fix it.

Within minutes Marla walked in with a syringe full of something she was determined that Brenda would take. "Bend over and give me a soft spot for the injection of its B12, an iron cacodylate."

"What the hell is cacodylate?" She queried.

I just told you now pull down your pants and bend over unless you prefer to have it in the arm, although there's much more fat on your lower half." She answered.

This kind of angered Brenda, "What are you talking about I'm not fat!"

"I'm just saying there's more fat on your buns and on your arm."

"Yeah, I guess you're right. However, give it to me in the arm in case someone walks in. I don't want to be embarrassed showing my ass."

They both laughed, it was sort of strange as they proceeded walking down the hallway to the nurse's station to see what their assignment would be for the day. They asked the head nurse where the lady was that was shot during the robbery and if she was still in a coma? And if she was still in room 309?

"No change yet, she is still in a coma and I bet the police are livid because the bank robber has all the time in the world to travel as far as he can get from Pleasantville, and the police can't do anything but wait it out." The head nurse replied.

"Well, they're detectives, I'm sure that patience is one of their better virtues, have you ever seen one throw anything like a tantrum? I'm sure they get agitated, but doesn't everybody? I think I will probably pound the desktop with my fist, but then why would it never do anything to me."

They looked at each other, begin to laugh, "We better get out of here before They put us in a room wearing a straitjacket"

"Well," Marla said, if we aren't a pair to draw to I don't know who is."

Marla got home that night and poured a glass of wine and took it into the living while waiting for Brett to arrive.

Brett walked to the front door expecting the smell of food cooking, but it didn't happen, "Marla are you home, of course you are the cars in the driveway."

"I'm in the living room sweetheart, grab a glass of wine and join me."

"Boy how things are changing, there was a time when I had a glass already poured next to where I would sit and food cooking on the stove, now you want me to get my own drink. Would you like me to prepare dinner?" He asked, Being facetious.

"No of course not, I thought if you don't mind, we could have leftovers there's plenty left."

"Yeah, that sounds good. It was really great last night, and I've always heard that it's even better the next day, we'll find out after I have my glass of wine." So how was your day sweetheart, lots of patience?"

"No, not really, much like the last shift and that's fine with me. I can always find something to do. What do you think about the bank robbery?"

Brett opened his mouth and laughed, "What brought that on?"

"I don't know, I'm just remembering last night and wanted your opinion. The police investigators were at the hospital this afternoon, they were checking in to see if there was a possibility the prime witness was out of her coma, didn't happen. She's down for at least 3-4 days. I know I watched it happen many times, and I'd rather see them awake. Have you ever been knocked unconscious?"

"What kind of question is that, sure I have, why do you ask?"

"Well, when you awakened, did you question what happened or where you were, well, that's what most patients tell me that they're in a state of confusion."

"What brought all this on, I thought we would drink our wine, and, in a few minutes, I'd warm up the stew, what do you think?"

"Are you seriously trying to take over my job, not gonna happen. Let's just sit here and sip our wine, there's plenty of time."

"Okay, you're the boss tonight." He said with a smile, "but that could change at bedtime."

Sue Brett Gardner Persaud. He was going after more wine, he instead put the beef stew on the stove soon it would be suppertime.

"You're right Marla, the stew is better the next day." Brett commented. "So, you're saying you didn't like it yesterday? She asked laughingly. "Come on, you know all about what I meant." He returned, wondering if she really thought that or was she just kidding?

The subject was changed, "well Mr. Conklin, how did your day go?"

"It went like every other day; however, I can't say it was boring. It's rarely boring where I work. Sometimes when it's slow. I get a little stressed but not often. You're really acting silly tonight. Did Somebody tickle your funny bone?"

"No, I'm just being silly. Maybe it's the wine, I don't know and can't recall anything funny happening at work. Well, let's finish the dishes, go into the living room, have one more glass of wine and wait for the news before we go to bed at almost 10 o'clock and I'm anxious to see if they found out anything more about the hold up."

During the news they announced that the lady that witnessed the bank holdup was still in a coma and probably would remain that way at least two or three more days, however, when she does awaken will she be cognizant enough to remember the bandits face? "I'm sure she will have plenty of company like family and of course the police and the FBI."

"That sounds much like the news last night, wouldn't you say?" Marla asked.

"Yeah," Brett returned, "let's finish our wine and hit the hay. Maybe we will play around a little before morning."

"Sounds to me like you have a plan must be something in the stew." She chuckled, "Okay, let's do it."

They cuddled and spent some time talking and a little lovemaking and fell asleep.

Tomorrow's a new day and it starts with a shower. Marla stayed in bed until Brett finished his shower, he soon entered the bedroom to ask a question. "Would you mind making the coffee while I shower and get dressed and then I'll fix breakfast."

"Of course, I will, there are some great benefits in buttering you up, just kidding." He included with a wink and a smile.

When Marla walked into the kitchen the coffee aroma filled the room. "It smells like you're making bacon. Is that what I smell sizzling in the pan?" She questioned.

"Well love, since you have plenty of fat in the pan, I'll have mine over easy, and oh, wheat toast if you don't mind?"

"Of course, not Sweetheart, anything your little old heart desires." He said. "Oh well in that case, scratch, breakfast, just kidding. We have work to do."

"So, we better get to it." She said with a big smile.

They finished her breakfast and Brett kissed her at the door. "See you tonight babe."

"I'll be here when you get home. Do you want me to start dinner?" She asked.

"I'll think about it and call you later when you get home from work, okay?"

As always, Marla met Brenda in the parking lot and walked into the hospital together talking about last night, Brenda saying how well her, and Charlie were getting along and she thought they were getting close to getting engaged.

"That's great, Brenda, you deserve all the happiness in the world, maybe someday you will someday have a double wedding wouldn't that be great?"

Their shift went well, and it even seemed to go fast. Marla stopped at the nurse's desk to use the phone, she called Brett," I haven't asked you yet, but what would you think about my asking Brenda and Charlie over for dinner, you can stop by the little Mexican restaurant and pick up some take-out and we can dine together, what you think?"

"Run it by Charlie and I'll do the same with Brenda. I'll talk to you at home."

"Okay, sounds like a wiener. I'll see you in Brenda's home. I think I'll take Charlie home so they can ride together in her car when they leave after we eat dinner."

"Great thinking Brett, see you at home, oh and I'll stop by the liquor store and grab a couple of bottles of wine."

Brett agreed with the request with the question, "Sweetheart when we go to bed tonight. I would like to have a discussion just a little conversation with you if you don't mind, don't stress out about it is nothing serious."

"No, of course I wouldn't mind sweetheart, why can't you tell me now?

She questioned. "It is something I want to discuss over the phone, Okay?"

"Sure, if that's what you want, am I in trouble?"

"No, not at all, but it is something we need to discuss in detail. I've got to go sweetheart. I'll be at our hacienda with an arm load of Mexicans, see you there."

Marla walked away scratching her head contemplating Brett's statement and wondering if perhaps she had done something wrong. She certainly couldn't think of anything, oh well, she'll just have to wait and see.

She approached Brenda saying, "You're going to have to follow me home. You and Charlie are dining with us tonight in our new home and Brett will follow Charlie home and ride to the house with him that way when the nights are over you too can ride home together in your car." Marla said like a drill sergeant.

Brett and Charlie were understandably late, after stopping at Charlie's and then the restaurant to pick up the food so by the time the guys got home the girls were on their second glass of wine, I wonder if perhaps that will be that topic of discussion in the bedroom tonight?

The dinner went well. Everyone enjoyed the change in menu, they didn't eat Mexican very often, so it was nice for a change. The girls now on their third glass of wine and the guys on their second. It wasn't long before dinner came to an end, they moved into the living room to talk, it didn't last long because all involved had to work the next day.

Well said Charlie, "I think we had better head for home tomorrow is another workday." He reminded.

Brenda gave little resistance; I think she might be enjoying the wine too much. She finally agreed it was time to go. They said their good nights at the door, Brett and Marla stood watching them leave. Then closed the door and headed towards the bedroom. Marla was anxious to hear what Brett had on his mind.

Once in bed they lay on their backs; Brett had his arm behind his head. "Well," Marla said, "what's on your mind that is bad enough we have to discuss it in bed?"

"The purpose of being in bed is irrelevant, it's just more comfortable. Well, what I'm concerned about is that we're drinking too much, and I don't want alcohol to change our lives we're beginning to rely on wine every night and if we're not careful we will become alcoholics and that's not the way we want to live our lives. Now we don't have to stop entirely, we can still enjoy one glass a night if that's what you want.

So, what you say?" Brett asked, he laid – back waiting for a response from his partner.

"If that's what you want Brett, and to make it easier for you I've had that same thought, but didn't say them because I thought you were enjoying the wine and yeah I fully agree with you, no more wine only on special occasions."

"Is there any wonder why I love you so much?"

With that being said they enjoyed a little hanky-panky, rolled over and fell asleep.

It was Friday morning, the possible witness to the bank robbery awoke from her coma, you can bet as soon as the word gets out, she'll be attacked by a flock of buzzards, known as the FBI.

And so, it came to pass, the lady was cognizant enough to attempt a description of the robber.

The FBI brought in a profiler and a sketch artist. She began sketching by description and by the end of the day they had a composite.

Back in the office of the FBI. They revealed the composite to the media and soon it was all over the news. Now if only the description was close enough for just one person to make a positive ID there was a good possibility the culprit would be found and brought to justice.

That night Brett and Marla made their final move to the new house, brought the last load of clothes and trinkets and were now ready to stay permanently.

"What we discussed last night, well since we were spending the first night in her new home. I guess a toast is in order, what would you say to a glass of wine?"

"Hello glass of wine we're going to celebrate tonight, and we must start by excluding your presence after one sweet glass. Beautiful moment, she lifted the glass, "Here's to your new house."

"Well, I'd say that was a little bit overdone, wouldn't you?" He laughed They hung up clothes that they brought from the old house, Brett suggested

They take a break and sip their wine in front of the TV.

The 11 o'clock news came on showing a sketch of the robber given to the FBI by the witness.

Brett said, "Look at him, that sketch looks just like Justin's father, but then it's not a photo, I could be mistaken, but there's definitely a close resemblance to Justin's dad, I hope I'm wrong because if I'm not, then I just hired a killer. There were two men in every robbery except the last one. One was older and larger and the other was smaller. Kinda fits a pattern. I hope I'm wrong, I really do."

"Oh, Brett, surely not. He appears to be such a nice guy but then, killers come in all shapes and sizes, so the nice guy statement could be a misconception." She corrected her statement.

"We'll have to be sure before I draw any conclusions, I wouldn't want to accuse Justin falsely sure would cause a lot of distention. Let's wrap it up and hit the hay. We both have to work in the morning. Oh, by the way, is it customary to consummate a new house as though it is a marriage?" He laughed. At work the next morning Brett met with Charlie in his office to discuss Justin's situation if there really is one. He wants Charlie to keep a sharp eye on Justin and to make sure there isn't any change in his mood after last night's TV announcement.

Justin waved as he walked past the office on his way the rear of the building where he did most of his work, didn't appear to be under any pressure, and that by no means that he's not.

Marla met Brenda at work and surprised her with the information that her fiancé may possibly be working with a killer. Needless to say, Brenda was shocked, she didn't believe it or didn't want to.

They continued their conversation while strolling down the hallway towards the nurses' station. "I can't believe all this from a sketch, wow, that's inconceivable, she continued, but certainly a possibility.

"Well, Brenda, I think we'll learn more if Brett gets the clues he's looking for, but he told me last night he would be careful not to cause suspicion around Justin if he is in fact one of the killers. There's no telling how he might defend himself, who knows Justin's might be carrying a gun. He said he would tell Charlie to keep an eye on him for any suspicious activity. However, at this point in time it is just a metaphor."

At the nurse's station Marla's assignment was a room 307 and an elderly male that had suffered a stroke, she would keep an eye on him and administer whatever drugs the doctor recommended.

Brenda, walking down the hall just before lunchtime stopped at the doorway entrance to room 307 spotted Marla. She went inside and asked her if she was going to make it to lunch or was she stuck with the patient, well I guess stuck is a pretty harsh word when tending to a patient, but after a few years, you tend to overlook the language and that doesn't mean you do any less for the patient, I think you just get used to doing yourself job.

Marla asked for a relief nurse, and Brenda walked to the elevator and down to the cafeteria for some of the nationally known hospital food.

They chatted during lunch. The topic of discussion was all about Justin and what if anything Brett found out about him and his dad.

Brett didn't want to corner Justin, that would be obvious, so he started off by wandering nonchalantly through the shop talking to each technician while he strolled around the shop.

Brett was intercepted by Charlie, curious as to why the boss was interviewing each and everyone in the shop. Charlie's question was answered. As Brett did his best to explain in a soft voice. He said, "I'm trying to work my way to Justin without causing too much suspicion."

"Okay Brett, everything appears to go smoothly."

Brett patted Charlie on the back then continued down the line of technicians. When he came to Justin he said, "How is your day Justin, are you completely comfortable with your job?"

"I'm doing fine, are you satisfied with my work?" He questioned.

"Oh yeah Justin, in case you are not completely familiar with the way I conduct business. I kind of ease around converse with each employee, just to see if they're happy with their jobs, encourage them to keep up the good work, no big deal. I may not come around for another month or two. Justin, keep up the good work."

Brett was not satisfied with the way he conducted his talk with Justin. He went back to his office to contemplate his next move.

At day's end Justin who had just passed in front of the office window, Brett motioned for him to enter the office.

"What's up boss?" Justin questioned, wondering why whatever Brett wanted he didn't ask him back in the shop?

"Is nothing in particular or anything about your work. It just came to me why I didn't ask about your dad, how's he doing? I haven't seen him in years."

"Well, I really can't say I haven't seen him for almost a week, but now that you mentioned it, I'll swing by on my way home. I'm kinda concerned about giving you a heads up tomorrow, okay boss?"

"Great, Justin, I hope you find him well after all, you once told me he attempted suicide twice and I hope that's not the case this time." Brett concluded his conversation.

With that, Justin said, "I'll see you in the a.m." was his last words as he left the office.

Brett closed up shop, he and Charlie walked out of the office into the parking lot together. "Well, Charlie asked did you get any unusual information from Justin?"

"I think tomorrow I might better be able to answer that question. I didn't want him to think I was interrogating him but I did ask about his father, he said, he hadn't seen or talked to him for the last for five days, I find that hard to believe since they used to spend a lot of time together, and all the sudden they quit communicating I really doubt it. I think he's covering up for his dad. That sketch was almost as good as a photo, as far I'm concerned, although I hadn't seen his father for a while. I have a vivid imagination of how he looked the last time I saw him."

"Do you really think he's a robber/killer?" Charlie asked.

"I do. I don't want to believe it, but if I'm correct, we have a killer for an employee." Brett stated.

When Brett arrived at his new home, Marla was waiting for him in the kitchen while fixing dinner, and of course a question. "Well Brett, how did the interrogation go, did you get the information you were seeking?"

He explained to her in detail, which was less than she expected. "But tomorrow is another day and I have plans laid out. What you say we go for a drive. After dinner I liked to cruise by Justin's dad's house, just to see if his cards were in the driveway and I'm betting it is not. Also betting that Justin doesn't even go by his place. Like he said he was going to do. I think he knows his dad is long gone but is afraid to admit it."

The phone rang, it was Brenda she sounded so excited she was having difficulty speaking the words out.

"Slow down Brenda, I can understand you having a problem with your family or Charlie?"

"Well, you know I always get a letter from my cousin in Texas. Well, she called, which she seldom does. She usually writes, but she said that the late news showed the sketch the lady had given the FBI, and would you believe it. Quote, 'A friend and fellow nurses stopped at the Cowboy's club, a local bar where a lot of women hangout and of course plenty of cowboys as well. You're not going to believe it, but the man in the sketch was sitting on the school stool right next to Peggy. That's my friend, and she was sitting right next to the man and was almost positive, was a man in the sketch. It was eerie.'" She said nervously.

"So, I ask, did you call the cowboys?"

"Are you crazy you don't mean the cowboys are the Texas rangers?" She corrected.

"Well, what's the difference between the Cowboys?"

"No dummy, you're talking about ranchers,"

"Well rangers, ranchers, cowboys. What's the difference, Call the police, call as soon as we hang up. Okay?"

"I guess, but I do want to get involved. I don't have time to go to the station for an interview." She explained.

"Oh, come on, just tell them you want to remain anonymous, but they can verify the information with the bartender, just be sure to give them the bartender's name that was working last night." Brenda said it was more like a command than the request.

She agreed to do as requested as soon as they hung up the phone. "His name was Doug Marlowe. He volunteered that he works almost every night so he should be in too hard contact."

They talked for a few more minutes, said goodbye and hung up the phone. "Well said Brenda we'll talk tomorrow. I guess she's going to contact the local yokels and give them the data. I'm sure they'll bust ass right over there to the barn and start the interrogation."

"All come on girl, they don't operate that way, do they? I've heard of the Texas Rangers and their good, but I don't think they would leak any information from someone, would they?" Marla asked. She knew better but wanted to play along for the heck of it. "Well I'll say one thing we have to keep our eyes open on the nightly news, it'll be interesting to see what develops after they talk to the bartender. But she expected it to be a few days before letting information out right away."

"You know what's scary, if it turns out to be the killer, and if it happens to be Justin's father, I'm afraid for Brett, I mean, when everything comes out of the open what do you think Justin will do? Will he do like his father and hightail it?" She queried.

"That would be terrible Brenda, but Charlie hopefully doesn't get involved or in line of fire. I didn't mean for it to come out that way. I don't want either of them to get hurt, you know, right?"

"Of course, I do. Marla, it's a frightening thing and you and I have to worry just like our group, we must think positive. Everything is going to come out all right." Marla said with conviction.

"I know, but it's still hard not to worry, after all, we've only been together a short time.

I wouldn't want to lose him now." Brenda said with a tear in her eye. "Since you and Charlie got together life has never been the same." Marla said being sympathetic.

Brenda asks, "Did you ever in your wildest dreams think we would be in this place only a few years ago when we vowed to remain celibate until we graduated from college and entered into nursing?"

"No," she replied, "I didn't but I am sure glad things turned out the way they did, didn't you?"

"Yeah, well, I think the best is yet to come, if that's possible."

That night Marla and Brett had a peaceful dinner and watched the news, nothing new. "I guess it's too soon to get any information on the robbery/killers, maybe tomorrow. You know, it felt really creepy when we passed Justin's dad's place and of course I never expected him to be home, but he is probably in Texas by now."

"I bet by the time the Rangers interview that bartender. He'll probably be in New Orleans, or somewhere other than Texas." Marla declared.

"Wouldn't be a bit surprised he can't afford to stay long in any one place, someone else is sure to recognize the sketch. It must be terrifying being on the run like that. Not knowing when the cop might pull you over. Looking over your shoulder constantly is a hard thing to live with, you think he misses Justin?"

"Yeah, but not enough to come back to Pleasantville, too much of a risk he'll be on the run for the rest of his life, you can take that to the bank."

That night they continued the conversation after going to bed, same conclusion. They were confident Justin's dad would never return on its own volition. If he ever comes back it'll be in handcuffs. One tender kiss and off to Slumberland.

CHAPTER 12

TO CATCH A THIEF

The next morning brought a sunny Friday and another workday for Brett and Marla. Although it was routine It was nonetheless a workday.

"Well," Brett said, "what should we do over the weekend? Are you up to a barbecue, the weather looks great too should be a good one? I don't know if you're up to inviting her but if you'd like we'll contact Brenda and Charlie, they could spend the night if they're agreeable."

"Sounds great babe, are we back on the wine list?" She conclude with a smile.

"I guess that's why I suggested they spend the night, I know they only live a few miles but if we're drinking and driving it just isn't safe, not even driving around the block, and yeah, It was my idea to quit drinking so much, we've been pretty consistent leaving it out of our daily routine however, once in a while is not going to hurt."

Brenda was already at the hospital parking lot when Marla came wheeling in, she had to park a short distance from where Brenda had parked, that's what happens when your late.

They walked into the hospital together, as they do every day. They checked into the nurse's station. Nothing astronomic, kind oft, same old same old. A few new patients, some with cuts and bruises others breathing to survive. One lady patient that had been in the hospital for months, she finally passed away and that's always sad for the nurses that tend to them. Although nurses are not supposed to become too close with their patients is difficult not to sometimes.

Marla and Brenda went home. "Do you and Charlie want to come over Saturday night for a backyard barbecue? Oh, and plan to spend the night. Brett thought because there would be some drinking. It would be better if you two didn't drive after the party was over."

"That's a smart idea, I'll run it by Charlie and let you know tonight, okay? Brenda asked."

Of course, Charlie didn't put up any argument. It's funny how Brett and Charlie worked together all day, five days a week, and yet they enjoyed being together on weekends. I guess we can attribute some of it to the longtime friendship between Brenda and Marla. They never get tired of each other's company even with the same set of circumstances. Brett and Charlie work the same shift every day as does Brenda and Marla.

Friday night Marla prepared dinner in her kitchen, when Brett walked through the door he commented, "Smells good babe what ya got a cooking?"

"Well, I believe you like Mexican so I thought you might like some chili and beans with cornbread, how does that sound?" she questioned with a with a smile.

"Mucho bueno seniority." He chuckled as he strolled over to where she was standing next the stove. He put his arms around her waist, kissed her fervently on the lips.

"I love your romantic nature, but don't hang onto me too long or I'll burn the cornbread. Take a seat at the island I'll pour you a glass of table wine if that's okay with you?"

"Only table wine, surely we have something better than that." He replied.

She poured his wine with a comment, "Aqui es un vasa de table." Not the perfect Spanish, but adequate

"Only table wine, surly we have something better than that."

"Just kidding, I thought I would return your Spanish." Marla said.

"Good job, now when is actually going to be ready I'm starving."

"Keep your seed, I'm just about to serve you a bowl, want butter on your cornbread?" Marla question.

"Sounds good to me sweetheart what's cornbread without butter?" He responded.

"Well, she replied, some people like to break it up in their chili, it's good that way, try it."

"I've had it that way before. It is good like that, you know, I have a cousin that puts cornbread and a glass of milk, disgusting. I prefer cake and milk, much more flavor."

"They both sound disgusting to me, are you sure you put cake in milk?" She questioned.

"Yeah, let's finish eating and go to the living room see if there's any news about our local robber/killer." He suggested as luck would have it, there was no new events on TV just the local news. Something about of fire, 70 miles north of Pleasantville so they watch the sitcom, been on for 20 years, don't you just love repeats?

Brett said, "This program is not worth losing sleep over, let's find something to do better. Like going to bed, we can talk about our plans for tomorrow night when our company arrives."

"Sounds good to me, is that all you have on your mind party, or perhaps you have something else in mind?" She chuckled.

"Are you suggesting a little Terpsichore around the bedroom?"

"Well," she responded, "will just have to wait and see. However, it might be fun dancing around the room." She laughed.

"With you, my dear fun dancing anywhere, the bedroom, shower, around the dance floor when your love most anything we do is most delightful."

"Oh Brett, you always say the right things. I'm so happy just to be in your presence and I truly love you when are we going to get married?" She asked with a smile.

"Soon my love, very soon, however, are you not content with the current arrangements?" He winked.

"Of course, I am, that piece of paper just makes it legal. So, we ever get divorced I'll get half of all you possess, and I hope you don't believe what I just said."

"Which part about being in my presence, or the divorce?" He looked at her with a look of concern, did she really mean that second part?

"We're talking gibberish, you know, I've always loved you and no piece of paper will ever change that. Let us change the subject. Get back to dancing around the bedroom." She said with laughter.

He took her by the hand and led her into the bedroom, no dancing, they fell asleep immediately.

The next morning was Saturday, no work for either tonight. There would be a barbecue in the backyard at Brett and Marla's house, of course Brenda and Charlie will be in attendance.

At 7 PM the guest arrived, and the party began. Brett had a large patio area were they could dance, and drink and they did all that switching partners occasionally. Finally, they set out at the dinner table fabulous barbecue consisting of steak, corn on the cob and a salad, makes me hungry just thinking about it.

By midnight the party came to an end was time for Charlie and Brenda to sleep in the new bedroom and a new environment. Although they were in the new house, only a week ago, this would be the first time they had an overnighter.

Says "good night" and entered their bedrooms. Three bedrooms were up a flight of stairs. However, when the group reached the top Marla said, "Your bedroom is at the end of the hall. It has its own bath and shower. There are towels in the linen closet so with that being said, we'll see you in the morning."

After another good night. They dispersed into their appropriate bedrooms.

The next morning Brett was first to awaken, he rolled over and gave Marla a kiss on the lips and headed for the shower.

Reached out and grabbed him by the arm. "Is it your intent to kiss me like that and leave me stranded?"

She was of course kidding, but Brett thinking she was being serious, climbed back into bed without resistance, they began a bedtime party. I bet Brett loves Marla's jokes.

After a shower. The two lovers dressed and went downstairs, Marla put on a pot of coffee," how long do you think they're going to sleep, maybe the aroma from the coffee awaken."

"I was thinking if they don't sleep all day, I would be like to take us to breakfast, how about that fancy little crowded downtown café. Would you like that babe?"

"I would Brett, but I hope we get there in time for breakfast, not lunch like my breakfast. It seemed like the rest of day. Just doesn't fall the place without starting the day with breakfast, however, can you skip breakfast No matter what time of day it is I have breakfast. It seemed like the rest of the day just doesn't fall in the place without starting the day with breakfast. How about you can you skip breakfast?"

"Sure, I eat when I'm hungry and need whatever suits my fancy." He concluded.

It wasn't long after the coffee was circumventing the house that two guests came bounding down the steps, it wasn't long for the coffee aroma circumvented around the house. Two guests came bounding down the steps, boiler coffee smells good. Brenda said, "You save a couple, Charlie and me?"

"You bet your life, and if you very drink it. I'm going to take for us downtown little café breakfast, sound all right, to you two?"

"Yeah, you bet we will be plenty hungry by the time we get inside the café as crowded as he gets on Sunday morning." Charlie said.

"Well, don't worry yourself about standing in line. I made a reservation for 11 AM so we had better get a move on it. If we don't show up on time will lose our place and have to stand outside in the line you are referring to." Brett said.

As luck would have it the wrong time and were seated immediately.

"Well, how did you to sleep last night?" Marla asked, "was your bed comfortable?"

"Yeah, Brenda. The question you remember when we went camping and flats, well bed kind of reminded me of that trip, sleeping arrangements. Don't get flustered. Marla just pulling your leg." Brenda explain with laughter.

"Oh Brenda, you are totally crazy, remind me to go camping with you again sometime." Marla responded.

"Okay you to the waitresses coming do you know what you want to order?"

"I do, Marla interrupted. I am having breakfast!"

"Yeah, I know we discussed that at home, but I'm having lunch thinking maybe chicken fried steak, with mashed potatoes and gravy." Brett said.

"That sounds good to me Brett," Charlie echoed."

"Well," said Brenda, "I'm with Marla. I can't start my day without breakfast, so breakfast it was."

They sat eating their meal and conversing mostly about last night's festival.

It is, and that they should get together again soon, all agreed.

About halfway through their meal and elderly ladies sitting at the booth across from them in an attempt to get up from her seat, dropped her cane, she put one hand on the table and bent down to pick it up when suddenly she fell to the floor. Charlie and Brett sitting on the aisle side of the table jumped to their feet to assist the lady.

Brett asked for the girls to come check out the lady for injuries them both being nurses were certainly qualified. However, the lady insisted she was okay, "Just help me off the floor, I'm all right." She insisted.

Marla was very determined of her assistance that they check her out. She had the lady move one leg at a time. She did so, moving the left leg first and then the right. However, she, while moving her right leg was in great pain. Even with the excruciating pain. She still insisted she was all right, but Marla was the doctor at this time and told Brett to go to the cashier and have him call 911. There was a battle mostly from the lady on the floor, but she would lose this one, the ambulance was pulling into the lot at this very moment.

Two attendants entered the café and made a quick analysis of the lady and brought in the gurney. They laid the lady on the gurney; she was still complaining that he was all right. But again, she lost the battle of the words.

The ambulance driver asked her husband if you wanted to ride with her to the hospital. Of course, he did and so soon the sirens screaming and red lights flashing.

Meanwhile, Brent's group returned to the table to finish their now cold food. They at least had another cup of hot coffee. "I wonder how old she is. And if she's healthy enough to withstand two and 1/2 to three-hour surgery?" Marla queried.

"I don't know," Brenda chimed in. "One thing for sure winner lose she can live much of her life with a broken hip, I wish her luck. Sometimes the elderly just doesn't have the stamina and often lose the battle."

"Yeah," Brett said, "I knew this guy whose mother fell and broke her hip, she never recovered, died following the surgery. Of course, she was 95 years old that many people at age survive that type of operation I understand."

A few days later Marla went to check out the lady in question, she was doing fine. Recovering well and would be released in a few days. Marla set next to her bed side and held her hand, she loved talking to the elderly patients and I'm sure they appreciated Marla's efforts.

The day went well. Not too many surgeries, or deaths, and she was happy with the progress. The elderly lady had made, as for tonight, Brett wondered when Marla might expect to be home. He never knew what she had in mind, wait and see was a daily slogan.

Marla said good night to Brenda and see you tomorrow. She then drove out of the parking lot heading towards home. When she arrived at the gate. It opened, Marla drove through and parked her car in the driveway. She went inside and out of instinct, she began to prepare dinner 30 minutes later Brett came through the gate and went straight to the kitchen where Marla had already poured the wine for both he and she.

"What are you cooking sweetheart, smells good."

"I'm trying, and experiment with stroganoff instead of beef. I'm using turkey just sounded good. And of course, a little different from the usual."

Brett sat at the island and watched her cook.

"Are you trying to steal my recipe?" She asked with a touch of laughter.

"I would know what to do with it if I did, you'll have to teach me."

"Oh, come on Brett, United cook as well as I do, in fact you could possibly show me a thing or two."

"Well, that may be true in some cases when it comes to cooking you win hands down."

After dinner they took the wine and went to the living room. "What you say to a movie?" Marla asked.

"Well, sweetheart you've got the control."

She tosses to Brett, "Not now, so come on and find us a good flick. We haven't seen a movie for quite a while, see if you can find a good murder mystery."

"Are you sure you want to ministry, the last time we watched one you are all over the bed trying to sleep, jump around, twisting back and forth. I thought I never would wallow sleep." He declared

"Maybe after they catch the Pleasantville killer, I'll sleep a little better, maybe less jumpy. I hope."

"Yeah, that this kind way, have you on your mind, especially not knowing if I'm working with a killer," Brett said.

"Gosh, babe, I really hope it works out for both you and Justin. It just seems so bizarre, he and his father it's not the way a family supposed to be. My family is so different we all enjoy each other's company. Thanksgiving and Christmas. The other day. I can imagine it being any different."

"Me neither. Life is too short to waste it by taking from others instead of earning it, storing it away for retirement. The life of a bandit is no life. Hello. Well let's see what we can find on the TV." Brett suggested.

He began to scroll through the channels, finally after shifting through five or six times. They agreed on a romantic movie, this just may turn into pleasant evening.

The movie ended in tears. Of course, Marla was more than just empathetic. She was willing to share her feelings and emotions. Throughout the entire movie, which of course was annoying to Brett because he could concentrate on what the movie was all about, too many distractions. However, he allowed it because that's what you do when you're in love with each other you give-and-take.

Just after the movie ended, and Marla and Brett getting ready for bed. There was a news bulletin about a man in Houston, Texas sitting at a bar. They wish to remain anonymous. The man in the sketch of the bandit was seen at the bar about 11:30 PM last night, it looks like he's on the move. Lead detective make any announcement said he will most likely show up again for leaving Texas, if you see this person do not try to apprehend him. He's known to be armed and dangerous. Before closing his statement, he gave a number to call or just call 911. They will direct the calls the proper authorities.

The FBI has been on the case since they robbed the First Bank, making it a federal offense.

"Well," Brett said, "I suppose our next notification will come from New Orleans."

"What makes you think that?" Marla asked.

"Because that's what I would do, I've always wanted to see New Orleans." He said with a raised eyebrow.

Marla was laughing, you do really believe that great minds think alike and that you two are a match."

"No, I just made a joke out of a bad situation but it's really my opinion, and I'm confident we don't think alike. I have yet to rob a bank and I doubt he's smart enough to run a tech company if he was, he wouldn't have to steal."

"The more we hear about this situation, the more I wonder about Justin, I'm thinking maybe I should buy a gun and keep it in my desk in the office."

"Oh, you are thinking that way are you, I mean do you even know how to shoot a gun?" She asked concerned.

Two days pass. There was another bulletin stating that the man in the sketch was seen heading in the direction of New Orleans. However, they still don't know the identity and the chase goes on. Brett heard about it on his radio while listening to the news in his office, he couldn't wait to get home until Marla I know was only coincidental, but Marla will inevitably make a joke about it saying I'm some kind of a visionary, or perhaps a soothsayer, I know she'll come up with something silly until it becomes a reality. And there's no telling where her mind will take her maybe and, in a tangent, who knows?

Brett didn't know if he should call the police about Justin or wait for the identification of the bandit. He really hoped he was wrong, and it turned out to be someone other than Justin Clark, senior if not he would make that call in a heartbeat. There is no time to pontificate about friendship, justice must be served at any costs.

Two days later on his way towards New Orleans. The suspect was pulled over from his past as a Highway Patrol could figure out was because of a light violation, which was confirmed by the officer's auto camera. When the officer approached the vehicle, he was met with the fatal shot to the face, killing him instantly. The killer now moved up to the top 10 on the FBI's list of suspects. That me just now a national search, someone will spot suspect Attorney men different no other reason than the reward. I wonder where the kill will turn up next after New Orleans where I'm sure he's on his way right now. I'm also sure the killers confident knowing they will never find him since he just murder the only possible witness, it eventually they all get caught. Of course, this news hasn't been released to the public yet, but you could bet when Brett hears about it. He'll have some major decisions to make, some facts and some speculation.

Brad asked, "Marla, the weekend is upon us, what would you say if I suggested going to Reno for the weekend?"

"Sounds good. I haven't been there for about three years, I have to warn you, I'm not much of a gambler, however, is fun trying to beat the odds."

Shall we ask Brenda and Charlie to go. I me will have separate rooms." Brett asking the form of a question.

"Of course, on I love being around Brendan Charlie don't know what I'd do without them, well of course are a few things we could do alone. On the other hand, you be spending your time at the poker table allow be playing armed bandits."

"Okay then, I'll ask Charlie, or you can just talk to Brenda while you're at work."

"Great," Marla said, "I'll talk to her at work today, when are we planning on going to tonight or tomorrow?"

"Well we might as well go tonight it's only a 3 hour drive from here." He declared so, their plans were set Reno. It was, there was only one thing they never considered. The road was perfect for driving until they reached Donner Pass and then the road was loaded with snow and ice. They had to pull over the side and put on her change and fortunately there was a man standing next to his car was broke down and he was dirty from working on it so he volunteered to put the mom for them for a nominal fee.

Brett didn't want to lay into the snow and get dirty that this close to Reno. So, they drove slowly for several miles until I came to a small casino about 15 miles from Reno where they had the change removed. There was still snow on the road, but it was drivable.

They arrived in Reno 1120 that morning, pulled into the hotel and paid the valet to park a car in order to bellhop to take their luggage into the Peppermill resort spa Casino, beautiful. They went straight to their rooms to unpack and hang your clothes in the closets.

The group hadn't eaten since early that morning where they drove through a drive-in restaurant and had a breakfast sandwich, but not to worry restaurants stay open all night. Inside the room was a small bar loaded with diffcrent bottles of overpriced alcohol, just about anything you wanted.

Marla opened the two tiny bottles of wine, one for the other for Brett. "Well, Brett said nothing like a tiny drink with a huge price which is kinda silly when the bars open anytime as a matter of fact, why don't you call Brenda and see if they're ready to go down to the casino. The drinks are bigger and half the price the bar."

They all gathered at the bar and ordered drinks. Brett said, okay let's go gamble for a couple hours I'm going to play Texas hold 'em, what about you Charlie you in?"

"No, I will look for a crap table. Kinda crazy, what about you Brenda?"

"Would you like to play?" Marla asked.

"Well, I'm game for anything, since I'm playing on Charlie's money. I tend to be a little tight when I'm using my own." Brenda said with laughter.

Marla said, "I think I'll try my luck, Aquino, you don't have to be smart to play. It is marked so many numbers on the ticket and the dealer calls out the numbers you get 3 out of six you get your money back, if you nothing, you lose. Now you can play miniseries combinations like 678 910. You can even play all 20 if you want to. However, the more numbers you play, the less chance of winning, It's kinda like bingo without the chips."

Three hours past the girls want a little and lost some, however, the free drinks were getting to them. In fact, Marla was loaded for bear, slurring through her words stumbling on her way to the keynote counter.

Brenda, who was slightly less inebriated told Marla that they should go back to the room for a while. While they could still make it up the elevator, but Marla was a bit difficult and insisted they gather their male counterparts before going to bed.

Brenda took Marla by the hand and assisted her while walking to work. Charlie was supposed to be at the blackjack table, it was like the blind leading the blind. When they got to the blackjack table. Charlie wasn't there in fact; he was nowhere to be found. They decided to go to the poker table where Brett was sitting in playing Texas hold 'em, he was running the chips through his fingers apparently ahead of the game and I don't think he was so happy to see them. He was winning, and when he saw Brenda holding Marla with both hands, well he wasn't a happy camper.

Brett finishes handed said," well fellows I guess I'll have to cash in looks like bedtime."

He got up from the table, took Marla by the hand and without saying a word, headed towards the elevators. The night was cut short, however, he won $370 for his efforts wasn't happy with the interruption.

There were two beds in the room. Brett thought Marla when she wakes up in bed by herself, would get the point missing her sleeping mate was very happy for her.

He took her clothes off down to her panties and bra Porter into bed and climbed into the other, perhaps he would get a better night's sleep. All he had was to come up for a reason. In the morning while he slept alone.

Brenda went to bed alone as well because he never found Charlie, who is not at the blackjack table, he was in fact across the room playing craps and doing quite well. After 3:30 AM, he decided it was time for bed, but where was Brenda? Charlie search the casino area from one into the other. But no, Brenda, so he concluded she could find her own way to their room and he headed for the elevator.

What are you the door he was surprised to find her in bed but unlike Brett Charlie climbed in beside her was sound asleep, and would never know he was there? She just kept snoring while Charlie wiggled alongside and fell asleep.

About 2:30 PM Brett rolled over on his left side, he kissed Marla on the lips while on the way to the shower. She jumped setting. Looking around the room trying to get her bearings, and then came the usual questions, "Where are we and why do I have such a headache?"

"Well, said Brett when Brenda and you drank too much. Now, I suggest we get the shower and I'll order is a couple of bloody marys, you remember a little hair off the dog?"

"Yeah, great idea. I remember it worked. The last time I suppose it'll work again was a try. I'd do about anything to get rid of this headache."

Marla took a shower while Brett called downstairs and ordered to bloodied, the waiter said, "I'll be there in a few minutes."

15 minutes later Brett thought to himself, stripping office T-shirt and shorts. He slipped into the shower. Surprising Marla, I think he had had a plan in mind, but then he did have a hangover.

Marla was shocked when she turned around. "Where's my bloodied?" She asked. She knew what he was after. It wasn't Mary, it was a Marla.

Brett finished showering and ran the towel vigorously over his body stepped out stall. Marla was still sitting on the side of the bed suffering from the alcohol pickling her brain.

Redhead barely pulled his pants up when early knock at the door. He reached in his pocket, pulled out some tip money, thank the servant and took Marla cure, hopefully.

She was setting rocking back and forth like she was cradling a baby when Brett entered the room, handing her the drink.

"Is that all she said, it's going to take more than one secure this headache!"

"Well, I'll tell you what you drink that one. And after you get dressed will go down and have another. There's a lot of time left in the day so if I were you, I don't back and not drink so much, will go into the dining room in order some lunch and have somebody eat out is that sound?"

He asked. "It sounds sickening, will give it a try."

By the time lunch was consumed. She was ready to take on the world. "I wonder where Charlie and Brenda are do you think their up yet?" She asked.

About the times words came out of her mouth in came their counterparts. They sat down at the table with Marla and Brett, who was halfway through lunch, I guess Brenda didn't drink as much last night as Marla, she looked cheaper ready to go this morning.

"I see you two are having bloody Mary's, Brenda said, little hair off the old dog? However, there's a problem with drinking too many each one tends to make you want one another. Think perhaps you better slow down. However, that's up to you if you like go to bed early." Brenda continued pushing the subject.

CHAPTER 13

MAN, ON THE RUN

They spent the next few minutes talking about what they were going to do after lunch. Brett said he was going back to the poker room and playing Texas hold em, had pretty good luck last night, hopefully it will continue today.

Charlie said he was going to pick up where he left off at the blackjack table.

"What about us Marla, keno again?" Brenda asked.

"Maybe later she answered. I think I'll go up to the room and take a nap. I'm still tired from last night."

They left the restaurant, each going in different directions. Brenda decided she was alone; she would play machines until Marla returned from her nap. She got tired of playing the machines and wandered over to the keno area. She sat there for about 30 minutes and I'd be damned if She didn't hit six a spot, it paid $1495. She was so excited she couldn't wait to tell Marla. She got her payoff and ordered a beer and went up to where Marla was sleeping like a dog, that wasn't going to stop Brenda she was too excited. She began pounding on the door until finally Marla answered in a grouchy mood.

"What the hell's all the pounding about?" She demanded.

It didn't take long to get her attention. When Brenda flashed $1500 in her face.

"Come on, splash some water on your face."

"Where in the world did you get all that money?" Marla questioned.

"I won it playing keno, $1500 I hit a six spot and when they called out that last number, I almost dropped my lunch. Come on, splash some water on your face and let's get going."

I suppose since Brenda won all that money she thought it would happen again, well it doesn't normally work that way especially playing keno. They say it is the worst odds in all gambling that craps are supposed to be the best, but we won't spoil her dreams. She'll find out on her own before the days are over.

Marla cleaned up, walked to the elevators together and down to the casino in search of another fortune, good luck with that.

They played for about two hours. Marla hit a ticket, 6 out of 8 which paid her $80 a little short of the 1500 Brenda had won. However, they enjoyed playing and they just knew their fortune was in the next ticket, which never happened.

Marla stood up with a beer in hand, said, "I'm going to find another game you want to come along?"

"No," Brenda said, "I can't leave a winning game." Some people never learn. "Okay, Marla said, I'll come back in a little while, have fun."

She wandered around the casino for a few minutes when a spinning wheel caught her attention. She put $20 in the slot and began to play. At first it didn't seem she would ever get anything and then something called the wheel of fortune, the big wheel began to spend when it stopped, she had won $350. Of course, that wasn't $1500 like Brenda had one, but it was sufficient, like they say is better than a sharp stick in the eye.

Gambling is strange, if you win, how much did you really win, well first count the money you started out with and deduct that from the winnings, how much does that equate to, not to be totally fair. What about the $250 hotel rooms and travel expenses well, perhaps that's a bit much. You can charge that for fun.

Saturday the four together had a late dinner and summed up their wins and losses. All things considered. Everyone had a good time and that's what it was all about, fun.

With Sunday still ahead. The group concluded they would stay and play until 4 PM Sunday and leave for home. It was only an approximately 3 Hour drive to Pleasantville. That is if Donner Pass was open.

After breakfast Sunday morning and of course your clothes pack is put on hold at the bellman's desk. They all went in different directions. Brett went back to the poker room. Charlie went back to the blackjack table and the ladies to the keno lounge. Marla decided to tag along with Brenda, who by now was sucked in like a magnet. Guess that's what happens when you win.

Marla only lasted for a few minutes before returning to the wheel when she won, as well. Once again, she got lucky winning more than $500. She quit and wandered back to where Brenda was sitting in grossed with keno.

Marla sat down next to Brenda and asked how she was doing.

She said, "Oh, I won a little bit and spent it trying to win more, how about you did you win anymore?"

Marla decided not to say anything about the winnings until the rest had declared Their winnings were losses, then she would spring it on them.

While driving up the mountain, heading home, Brett spoke first, "Well guys I don't know who won or lost, but I think we all enjoyed ourselves. Win or lose."

"Yeah," Charlie followed, "I did fair. I didn't really count the dollars, but I think my winnings came to somewhere in the neighborhood of $500 to $525 somewhat better than yesterday."

"I think Marla enjoyed herself except for Saturday morning. It's funny while playing you don't realize just how much alcohol you can consume, I'm sure she can attest to that, right Marla?"

"Oh, come on you guys, did you have to bring that up? I was trying to forget it. However, that bloody Mary sure did its job. However, when you come around to the alcohol it does calm the situation, but by the same token it makes you want another drink until you're right back where you started from. I stopped after the second lease for about four hours, but I had a beer, stuck to beer the rest of day. It doesn't seem to reach the brain as fast as vodka." She concluded her statement without divulging how much money she had. She planned to hold up for the rest of them to declare their winnings.

Brenda spoke next, "Well I guess I'm the highest winner. I won $1500 on keno so I guess tonight's dinner is on me, isn't that the way goes." She asked.

"Well, Brenda, we haven't heard from your counterpart yet. How about Charlie, did you really win $500 or are you just putting us on?" Brett asked jokingly.

"Okay, Charlie said, "$500 is still less than $1500. However, you made more than me Brenda so I can come in second. Of course, we haven't heard from Marla yet, "What about Marla, how much did you get away with?"

"I guess I come in third with $350 so I'm in for a free dinner, right?" "Okay, Brett said, it looks like we were all winners, so I guess we all had a good time when she says guys?"

"You're right Brett will have to do it again one of these days. However, we don't want to make it a habit but a couple of times a year shouldn't be considered habitual."

Four hours later, they pulled into the small cafe on the outskirts of town, it was dinner time, and everyone was ready. They climbed out of Brett's car and walked into the café, took a booth next to the window and soon a waiter came to take their order.

After dinner they drove to Brett's home where Charlie had left his car before going on the trip. Charlie and Brenda climbed into his car, said thanks for the fun weekend and drove away to their home. It was time to prepare for tomorrow, work for all.

Once again, the now serial killer was spotted at a bar. Seems to me he should stay out of bars or just turn himself in, it will happen eventually.

It became obvious to the killer that the person sitting next to him was scanning him trying to ID him. This caused fear and although he had just arrived in New Orleans. It was again time to hit the road.

This was no ordinary fugitive. He was smart and usually thought outside the box, this time was no exception.

It was time for him to leave, get out of Dodge.

Most often on the run he would steal a different car, but this time he hid out until 3 AM and stole the license plates from a local vehicle thinking even though the police were looking for the car he had stolen a few days prior and looking for Texas plates, not Louisiana.

He drove to the outskirts of town, topped off the gas tank and headed out of the area on Highway 287 towards Colorado Springs. He probably wouldn't make it without some sleep. It was at least a 20 Hour drive.

Occasionally a state trooper would speed by him with the red lights and sirens screaming, but no pullovers. But I bet he would be wiping his brow, must be a terrible feeling knowing that the next police car that approaches could be the fatal blow. Find a dark place off the highway at sleep during the day and drive by night, stopping at every rest area he came to. After relieving his bladder, he would cautiously stroll around until he needed to stretch his legs after sitting for hours behind the wheel. The last stop he found a cap inside one of the stalls looks like a good idea, it also helped to hide his baldhead as it appeared in the sketches, can't be too cautious when on the run.

With his twisted mind it makes one wonder if he ever thought of his son back in Pleasantville, I'm sure he did, in fact, the main reason he went on the run was to protect his son. That's only speculation, but it's possible.

He passed through the city looking for a dark side of town. He was searching for a cheap motel out of sight of too many people. He didn't drive all the way to Colorado Springs just to be caught. I know he was somewhat jumpy, and you can't blame him for traveling through Dallas where he had been spotted there once and didn't plan on it happening again. He thought it was safe to bypass Dallas and head on to Amarillo, but that was behind him. He was in Colorado now looking for seclusion, somewhere to hide until he felt it was no longer safe.

Justin senior could not gamble on robbing a bank and soon his funds would decline to a precious few dollars and he would be forced to rob something, but nothing as big as a bank. After all, even though he lives in a cheap motel, he had to keep the rent up.

He would drive around the outskirts of town casing joints that didn't carry a lot of money like banks, but enough to get by on.

At work Brett noticed Justin was a little on the anxious side, probably seen the same news bulletins that most people saw. If so, he has figured it out and you can bet Justin will disappear soon.

There's one thing the bandits were unaware of, police know the make and model of the stolen car, he's aware of that, but he is depending on the Louisiana plates to give him cover. However, he doesn't know about the missing tail light which is on the police camera that he shot and killed and if that information is out on the police department across the country, and you can bet they are. If he's pulled over for a mechanical violation. Now the officer knows not to approach the vehicle without his gun drawn. Of course, one more murder won't change his sentence, I'm betting on the death penalty. It's unlikely the judge would commute the death to a life sentence without the possibility of parole, not for murdering a police officer, no way.

I think it's narrowing down to when or where and, what state our friendly bandit will be in for his final count.

He drove around the city outskirts looking for a store with a single operator, and especially those that close at midnight. There was a small market just on the edge of town. I couldn't imagine the store keeping more money than a bank in this out of town market, but killers and beggars can't be choosers and he was getting desperate.

Three nights in the early evening he would drive past the store casing activities, like the clerk and his pattern. He noticed that the clerk closed every night 10 minutes before midnight. He would lock the front door, take the trash out the rear door to the trash bin. Which is in the dark alley just outside the door. On the fourth night the bandit had begun waiting just behind the door on the outside of the building. The clerk will open the door and he wouldn't see his attacker. As soon as he opened the door, turned towards the trash container the robber/killer hit the clerk in the back of her head with the, butt of his gun, the clerk would never know just how lucky he was.

The bandit went to the cash register, which was open and ready to put the money into the safe. But not tonight. The bandit grabbed the money and was on his way to the motel before the clerk knew what hit them. By the time the police arrived, it was all over but the handshake and of course, the customary event would still be in play like gathering evidence, that is, if there was any together.

It would be ironic if the killer was caught because of the taillight and it could happen, at some time or another his luck will run out.

Monday morning Brett went to work right on schedule. He met Charlie in his office where he told Brett that Justin hadn't shown up for work, yet it was already close to 9 o'clock and Justin has never been late before, at least since Brett hired him a few months ago.

"Well Charlie, let's give him some time almost anything could've happened. Like his car might've broken her something to that effect, and then being realistic."

"He could snap and slip out of town just like his father did."

"Do you really think that Brett? I mean he's been under scrutiny ever since you hired him, but I wasn't sure you believed it. If someone would identify him, we could be more positive about Justin."

Tuesday, Justin was still a no-show. Brett decided to drive around in Justin's neighborhood and converse with some of the neighbors to see if they knew anything about him disappearing. The information Brett had on him was in his resume, never really never knew Justin's that well so it would be somewhat difficult to approach the police or make a phone call to the police. They may laugh him out of the park, I mean I really don't have anything other than suspicions that will not go far with the police. Probably laugh him out of the park.

Brett, talked to people that live close to Justin's house, but nobody seemed to know anything. Across the street and down the block a lady actually knew Justin, so first thing she told Brett was that they had an affair several months ago until she kicked him out and gave him an alternative. She decided her life with her family was more important than an affair with Justin. She told Brett his car was home Friday night and she noticed it on her way home from the mall. However, it was gone Saturday morning when she went to work. She worked at an animal clinic and they were open seven days a week.

Brett was satisfied that his one-time friend Justin, was on the run like his father.

He notified the police, but his story was a hard sell, they told him they needed something more positive, that his evidence was a little too weak. They would launch an investigation any way they had to investigate any clue they got.

Nobody knew how Justin and his dad made contact, certainly not by phone, too easy to trace. There's a possibility that it was in a letter that would be my best guess. He not only made contact in some form with his dad, but they were on their way to meet up somewhere just to figure out where.

Justin left Friday night and could've possibly passed Brett's group on the way to Reno. However, Justin wasn't going to Reno. He drove straight through to Winnemucca where he spent the night at the casino hotel and even did a little gambling. And why not only Justin knew where he was going and nobody was looking for, yet.

Mr. Clark was almost playing cat and mouse games with the police, they were almost catching any would get away and would allow him freedom was kinda like Wiley and the coyote in the roadrunner, but eventually Wiley for the first time would corner the roadrunner.

Justin left Winnemucca the next day, not in any particular hurry, he would cross about 40 miles of Oregon before making his way to Idaho to meet up with dad.

About three hours passed, Justin came to an area where the highway made a sharp left turn. There was an old café on the corner. Justin decided to stay for a late lunch, a big mistake. The place was like a hangout for delinquents, Hicks to say the least. He ordered a sandwich, hoping the Cook had enough brains to make it. But then, how hard would it be to put two slices of bread together over some meat and cheese, perhaps a little mayonnaise and mustard. Sandwich turned out to be well put together and Justin enjoyed it immensely. So, he went over to the waitress with a tip for the cook, good job. He asked the waitress directions to Nampa.

She pointed to the road leading that way, big deal never said a word.

There was only one direction. From that point the lessee wanted to go back from whence he came. He paid the waitress and left her a hefty tip on the table exited the building and drove away in the direction the waitress pointed the path to Nampa to meet his father who was already at the cheap motel waiting for his son's arrival.

Two days earlier. Senior drove west on Freeway 84 passing a offramp to Boise, however, a police officer entered the freeway going in the same direction. The officer's jaw dropped when he noticed the car that just past all police departments in at least five Western states from Louisiana to West were alerted with a description of the car including the tail light out. Who would've thought that any apprehension of a killer the taillight would be a dominant factor in the apprehension of a killer?

The officer called the department and notified them of his pursuit that D cleared that he wouldn't attempt to capture the assailant rather follow him to see where he would ultimately stop for the night, for dinner. He would keep in contact with the FBI and inform them of the location. The plan was to survey Justin senior until he stopped moving and would at that point turn the report over to the FBI, they would take charge at that time and hopefully wait him out in case his cohorts showed up. They would then move in and apprehend the killers and get them off the streets.

There was however a problem, because they're wanted for crimes in four different states. However, the FBI only knows the crimes committed in some states, yet, the younger of the two was only involved in California. That by no means makes his investigation any less delicate. Even if Jr's crime turns out to be guilty by association. He will be judged accordingly.

The officer followed the killer past Nampa to a small-town west of the city. He was wondering how much further the assailant would go, would he try to Montana in his quest for freedom and then it happened, the bandit turned right on the ramp's final destination.

There was a small motel just around the corner that continued around an almost circle by running along to the east, paralleling the freeway. He pulled into the parking lot of this rundown motel parking with the office to check in. It was just an assumption by the officer that he had already made reservations.

Mr. Clark stepped out of the office, climbed under the wheel of his car and moved in front of the room where he would be staying for how long. Nobody knows. He took his luggage inside the room. After scanning the area, making sure he wasn't being followed.

The officer parked down the street to surveille the killer/bandit. He called the FBI and told them the location where he was staying.

Soon a car pulled up behind the officer and said they would take it from here that the officers did want in case the bandit assistant/showed up. He would notice the marked police car and possibly turn and run.

The FBI agent said in his car, hoping the other killer would show up and they can both be apprehended at the same time.

Just before 8 o'clock a young man pulled into the parking lot, went into the office briefly, then walked to the room where his father was waiting with a beer in hand.

Mr. Clark hugged Justin. They stood silently in an embrace like normal fathers, sons with these two were anything but normal.

Meanwhile, the agent said in the vehicle contemplating their next move. Lynn Vogel, one of the agents said, "John called the office and asked for backup and came in on the unmarked car we want to be sure not to allow these guys to make a run for and hopefully we won't get into a gun battle we want to capture them alive."

"Dammit," John said, "I'm looking forward to the interrogation. I really want the father to explain why he would pull down his own son, getting into bank robbing and murder. What kind of a man does that?" John concluded.

Seems thanks to Brett notifying the local office of the FBI that they were indeed Father and son, Justin Clark's and his son Junior's identification after all this time and all the six sending out the sketches to all of the states from Louisiana to all states west. Brett took a lot of doubt and abuse from the local and FBI in an attempt to positively identify and make the case of Justin Junior but after some investigation they were finally convinced was indeed the right two.

CHAPTER 14

THE CAPTURE

The two agents went around to the rear of the building hiding behind the room occupied by the killers. The back of the room was in the alley and in the bathroom was a small window allowing access to the two desperados. They were going to allow anything to get in their way. Not now nor ever, Period. Everything was set into place. After many machinations. A plot was finally positioned. They would wait until after 3 AM thinking the assassins would be asleep after a long venture across the states.

At 3 AM they moved in, announcing that they were FBI agents. However, they never waited for a response but instead kicked the door and with guns drawn, locked and loaded.

The assailants simultaneously set up in bed, unaware that anyone had knowledge of their location, and neither folder guns. It seems the element of surprise worked out when a shot was fired. It would make one wonder why Mr. Clark didn't attempt to draw his gun knowing his life was over. Some criminals knowing those circumstances would prefer to be shot down as to face the death penalty or even a life sentence.

Well, it didn't happen that way, after cuffing the two Justin Clarks wanted time they were allowed to dress after their clothes were checked out for weapons. They were put into the rear seat of two different cars driven by FBI agents and would soon be on a plane back to Pleasantville and incarcerated to wait a trial before a grand jury if the district attorney determined there was enough evidence to go before the grand jury and get an indictment. Without a doubt in this case, they would fall under the letter law.

The capture of the Clarks was all over the news and Brett didn't miss a moment of it. He in some way felt himself as part of it, all because he knew the Clarks personally, perhaps he felt guilty by association. And of course, that's nonsense.

"Okay Brett looks like a celebration is in order." Marla suggested.

"I really don't think a party would be appropriate under the circumstances, and from my perspective it's really sad. I mean, I've known these two for many years and talking to a priest would be more appropriate.

"I never knew you were religious or Catholic for that matter. It's funny after all these years we don't know what each other's religious affiliations are, we'll have to know before our wedding day." Marla questioned.

"Well soon their journey will come to an end, but they will either be executed or spend the rest of their lives incarcerated. I don't think the old man will be able to stand it being locked up for life." Brett said.

"What you think you really do about it, suicide?" She questioned.

"I'm sure the guards will keep a close eye on them and they won't let them off the hook that easily. They will make sure he lives. Artisans in full, whatever it is!" Brett explained his theory.

"Yeah, I suppose you're right. After all, the police and FBI went through a wasted year. They probably feel vindicated in their quest for justice, I know I would, under the circumstances."

The agents decided to take the two back to Pleasantville by police van, they might've flowed into Sacramento would drive them to Pleasantville by car, although it was faster by plane, They didn't want them exposed to the public and its only about a 9 Hour Dr. They will be better protected and easier to keep an eye on than on an airplane exposed all the other passengers.

When they arrived in Sacramento, they turned the bandits/killers over to the sheriff office where he held them in the county jail until the agents could talk with the prosecutor giving him all the evidence they had to take for the grand jury. There was little doubt they would get the indictment.

There were only nine jurors at trial, which is sufficient for the hearing that would decide if they would move forward with a trial or not, I'm betting there is.

It took the jurors only three hours after hearing the evidence to send their decision to the judge, and there would be a trial.

It would take place in federal court. However, for the time being. The calendar was full for at least three months and that meant he would not only be incarcerated but will be guarded.

It may not be hard to understand that Clarks Senior after killing as many as four people that his life was over, so why put it off. However, the guards were about to let anything happen to either of them. Not now, not ever.

Now Junior, although he was guilty as his father thought, perhaps dad would get them off of the hook by claiming he was the mastermind and his son never killed anyone, fat chance, but who knows anything could happen, it has before.

The two were not allowed to communicate in any way shape or form both in separate cells. I'm not sure they wanted to talk to each other of course, they were family.

For some of us 90 days is a long time, but not if you're in the Clarks shoes. Time is strange, and has many effects, for instance, if you're in a hurry. Time stands still and on the other hand, should you be awaiting trial like the Clarks. The clock strikes swiftly.

On Tuesday, 14 June, the trial would begin. It lasted only eight days for the jury to decide guilty on so many fronts. I would by no means be able to name them all I know for counts of murder and kidnapping, aggravated assault, hit-and-run homicide, and the beat goes on.

Brett duty is called to the local police, saying that he not only knew the Clarks Junior actually work for him and thought he was sure Justin Junior was part of the total crimes connected at least to those crimes in Pleasantville and there were many. It would be a week before the Clarks would know their fate. Perhaps even longer depending on the time the judge had, and he would be pronouncing the sentence not the jury, and that only means if they stand up and plead guilty to avoid the death penalty.

Brett came home from the trial about 6;30 that night because of the evening traffic, yet it was only 65 miles.

Marla greeted Brett at the front door with the normal 20 questions, but Brett came home prepared for the inevitable and answered her question one at a time. He told her not only was it a day of satisfaction but yet very sad. "It's hard to see someone you've known for many years whose life may possibly come to an end. Since the first time I became aware of these accusations I had a tough time coping with it, but life is life for some it goes on." He concluded.

"Oh Brett, guess what Brenda's pregnant!"

"Say what, pregnant. How did that happen, I withdrew that question? I think I meant how she knew she looked fine a week ago."

"Well Hans, it's only been over probably four weeks. She won't show for a while, I'm sure this is not something she would joke about." Marla declared.

"You know I've been wanting – your question for some time now." He said with a smile on his face as he got down on one knee and asked, "Will you marry me?"

Marla was shocked, although she knew she would one day, but this was totally out of left field. "Of course, I'll marry you, why did it take you so long to pop the question?"

"I guess just knowing that Justin's life was over and how young he was made me realize we were wasting time. If we ever have a family, it's time we got started. We let it go on too long, don't you think?" Brett questioned.

"Sweetheart, why don't we have a double wedding, I mean we have great friends, Charles and Brenda, why not do it together?" She asked to be serious.

"Well I'll tell you what? Friday. Why don't we have them over for the weekend and we can discuss it, have a barbecue, a little wine, what do you think?"

"I think I love you, you always come up with great ideas, and they usually work, and I believe this one tops them all."

"Thank you, for being in my life, but don't say anything to Brent at work or any other place. Let's make it a complete surprise."

"You've got it partner, I promise to keep my mouth shut, and that won't be an easy task for me." Marla concluded.

Both Marla and Brett kept silent during their time at work, nothing was said to Charlie or Brenda. This would be a total surprise for all.

Finally, Friday Brett asked, "Charlie would you and Brenda be onerous with your company? Marla and I would enjoy your company over the weekend for a barbecue and just any weekend. You're always welcome."

"Brett, I don't think Brenda has anything planned but I'll run it by her tonight and give you a call, okay?"

Charlie made the call stating, "It'll probably be too late for a barbecue tonight and we can't get there until around 8:30, how about we come then and eat light and wait till tomorrow to have the barbecue, what do you think Brett will do?"

"Sounds good Chuck, I will be awaiting your arrival."

They popped in at 8;15 a little sooner than expected, but then they had almost 3 days to have a barbecue and a great conversation. The four gathered around the island in the kitchen and Brenda asked, "Well Brett, did you hear the rumor?"

"I'm sure he did return, you don't think Marla could keep her secret of that magnitude do you, how far along are you?" He questioned.

"Well, it's just a guess, I haven't been checked out yet from a pediatrician, but I guess 3 to 4 weeks. I really don't know. Just a guess on my part."

"Well if you didn't know for sure could you have a glass of wine since you don't know if you're pregnant or not. I am sure it happens all the time." She looked at Marla seeking an answer to Brett's question. Marla just raised an eyebrow and shrugged her shoulders.

"Well," Brenda said, "if I didn't know that. I guess life would be as normal as usual, so pour the wine." She said with a touch of laughter.

They all enjoyed a glass of wine while Marla warmed up some leftover stroganoff, made a salad and that would hold them over until breakfast.

Gathered in the living room. They all sat with wine in hand while Brett surfed the channels on the TV. "Someone stop me when you see something you would like to watch."

"No, I'll tell you what, tell them the plan, that is if they'll go along with it. What we earlier discussed." Brenda looked at Charlie, who had yet to ask for her hand in marriage. I think he was dumbfounded and a little embarrassed. That the two had been together for so long and he had yet to pop the question.

Now he felt he was in the corner and had to say something. "Okay sweetheart we've loved each other for a few years now and under the circumstances, it sounds like a good time to tie the knot. What would you say if you marry me and make me the happiest guy in the world? I didn't come prepared with a ring, but I bet we can pick up one tomorrow."

"Well," Brenda said, "I have course, except that we were in love. I would say since the first we met and I'm certainly willing to have a double wedding, save lots of money. Just kidding. We have all been together for so long. Yes, I'd say let's do it."

"Okay to start with, Brett proposed to me today." "Did you accept?" Brenda interrupted.

"Of course, I have been waiting for this day for a long time, there's no way I would turn down his offer." She continued, "Brett and I want you to join us in a double wedding, you are planning on getting married are you not?"

"Well," Brenda said, "I have of course, except that we've been together and in love for such a long time, I would say since we first met and I'm certainly willing to have a double wedding save lots of money, just kidding. We have always been together for so long and yes, let's do it."

Silence filled the room, waiting for someone to speak up agreeing or disagreeing with the suggestion.

Brenda looked at Charlie who had yet to ask for her hand in marriage, I think he was dumbfounded and a little embarrassed that the two had loved each other for so long and had yet to pop the question. Now he felt he was in the corner and had to say something.

"Okay sweetheart, we've loved each other for a few years now and under the circumstances, it sounds like a good time to tie the knot, what do you say you marry me and make me the happiest guy in the world? I didn't come prepared with a ring but I bet we can pick one out tomorrow."

"All right, Brenda said, I have of course, except that we have been in love for a long time and I would say since we first met and I'm certainly willing to have a double wedding, save lots of money. Just kidding. We have all been together for a long time, and yes, let's do it."

Brett announced, "Tomorrow. Charlie and I will shop for rings. Since neither of us gave it a thought but will solve that problem tomorrow for sure."

"What about Brenda and I? We have to buy rings to, can we just all go together at the same time?"

"Sure, I see no reason why not, do you Charlie?"

As it turned out soon after breakfast. They all climbed into Brett's car, and went shopping. They went. On August 21 Brett and Charlie rented the town hall, which was rented out for parties, and this would be a huge one.

The Fletcher's, Marla's family and all of the relatives including their son from Elko, Nevada and his family and of course, at least a dozen nurses and a couple of doctors scattered in from the hospital. After all, Marla and Brenda had worked with them for years.

Brenda's family came with many invitations for their family members and friends, there were 69 and all plus a small band and the preacher, can't forget the preacher.

The wedding and reception lasted past 2 AM for the brides and grooms lasted a little longer. They enjoyed their honeymoon in Taiwan, one week and back to the old grind. When the happy couple is home and back to normal.

THE JOURNEY

The time had passed for the sentencing of Clark's. Mr. Clark had his attorney talk to the prosecutor he wanted to cop a plea, but only if they would reduce the distance to life in prison was 20 years of necessary, but no death penalty, please.

Seven prosecutors have no way we can accept a plea for reduction of sentence. We don't need the plea, we have all the evidence we need to convict, and I personally want to see this man executed never to get out of the streets again by any means.

Justin received a life sentence without the possibility of parole, I guess. Daddy didn't come through for his son. After all, the jury would ask for an appeal and he was mad at dad and wanted revenge by pleading his case that being his father was the instigator and drugging him along with them. But after Junior was convicted of two murders for kidnapping a woman in the first robbery, there was little chance of inventing the court that dad was completely alone in those crimes. Dad may have influenced his son, but he did put a gun to his head. They would serve a sentence. San Diego temporarily at the Metropolitan Correctional Center, Soviet but of course later on. Mr. Clark would be transferred to San Quentin to await the death penalty by lethal injection.

Life went on for wedding couples. Brenda had a little girl, she named her Melinda and Shirley after the middle of the following year, Conklin's had a boy they named him after Marla's maiden name, Fletcher and Brett's father, Cameron. Fletcher Cameron Conklin, Kind of cute wouldn't you say?

Both families a new journey has begun, raising a family and all in all their lives were lived as predicted, now that they had completed college in a few years serving General Hospital. Their lives were now complete. All that was left was moving forward. As for the Clark's a journey is ended to a certain degree, however they have a new journey, but somewhat less so look forward to.

There are journeys in everyone's life but of course, all are different. For example, a journey can be to do national work, or a trip overseas. Like everything in life, it all comes to an end. As for Brenda and Charlie they're still looking into the future. Our journey will end.

www.ingramcontent.com/pod-product-compliance
Lightning Source LLC
LaVergne TN
LVHW091548060526
838200LV00036B/745